MW01127049

ISBN-13: 978-1987863376
ISBN-10: 1987863372

Other books by Shyla Starr:

Persuasive Billionaire BWWM Romance Series

Stacey is trying to keep a handle on her life the best that she can. She is on the verge of losing her job and her apartment, while taking care of her sick grandmother. Her life takes an unexpected turn when she meets Charlie, who works for the construction company that is attempting to persuade her to move out of her home.

Tenacious Billionaire BWWM Romance Series

Adalia is too proud to accept help from the billionaire playboy, Trent Dawson. How long can she maintain her resolve? The bank is at her heels to repossess her business. To make matters worse, Adalia finds suspicious evidence of Trent's philandering ways. She must determine whether to trust Trent with the fate of her business and her heart.

Lonely Billionaire Romance Series

Tricia was hired to care for billionaire John's wife, who is dying. An unlikely romance emerges after his wife, Rebecca, gives John permission to pursue his happiness after she is gone.

Ardent Billionaire Romance Series

Deirdre doesn't know what to make of the gorgeous man that seems to be interested in her. His name is Parker Walters and he seems friendly enough. There is just something off about him. Why is he trying the hide the fact that he is the heir to his father's billion dollar software empire?

Fervent Billionaire BWWM Romance Series

Alexandra had never been with a white man before. She had seen William at the café before but she always kept her distance. It was unfortunate that their first chance meeting happened when she dropped her breakfast and spilled coffee all over his expensive business suit.

Audacious Billionaire BWWM Romance Series

Chante is torn between staying close to a man beyond her league, and fleeing from him to spare herself from a hopeless position. But she finds she is propelled into a place where she needs to confront her doubts and cast her fate aside to follow the dictates of her heart. Damned if she does and miserable is she doesn't, how will Chante face the events that will lead her to a place of pure happiness or to the pits of a broken heart?

Get the latest update on new releases from the author at:

https://shylastarr.com/newsletter/

This book contains all the stories of the "Elusive Billionaire Romance Series"

1 - Suspicion

Billionaire Hendrick is trying to repair his company's image by putting in some volunteer work, building a school and hospital for the impoverished children in Africa. There, he meets a beautiful African American volunteer, Jocelyn. They hit it off right away but does she belong in his world?

2 - Love Belated

What had Jocelyn done? Why was she being a fool by falling in love so soon? Not trusting her feelings, Jocelyn decided to return home and immerse herself in her work. Perhaps if she kept busy and dated other men, she can forget Hendrick. Things seemed to be going well and a wedding date with her man, Tim, was set. Nothing was going to ruin her day...until a man she was trying to forget shows up the night before the wedding.

3 - Love Amiss

Finally, Jocelyn started her new life with her chosen man. Was it the right decision? At one point or another, she was in love with either Tim or Hendrick. How could that be? The birth of her daughter, Jasmine, was supposed to ground and solidify her marriage. Instead, her partner's jealousy over her past relationship loomed overhead like a dark cloud.

Elusive Billionaire Romance Series

Books One to Three

By Shyla Starr

Table of Contents

Book One – Suspicion

Chapter One

"**I WANT** to know who the hell is responsible for this mess!" boomed Hendrick from the front of the boardroom.

Silence filled the room as all the top people in the company stared at Hendrick in awe. They knew he wasn't the kind of guy to be messed with. Considering the company had just been charged with federal and criminal charges for dumping industrial waste into the Arctic Ocean, they knew it was best to stay silent.

"I return from vacation to find the prosecutor in my office to tell me that a company that I built from the ground up to help humanity is being accused of filling the ocean with waste! Waste??" He screamed across the table, his face turning an angry red. Hendrick stopped for a moment to compose himself and looked at each person at the table, assessing their worth.

"Pray it was not one of you frontrunners that made the decision to handle the waste of the company in this manner. Now go, and I expect reports hourly about how we are making this right and where waste should be going from now on."

Everyone got up from the table quickly and filtered out of the room. Hendrick watched them all leave and turned to his right-hand man, Geoffrey, the CEO of the company.

"Tell me you didn't know."

A broad-shouldered man, Geoffrey held an imposing frame that fit well with the red beard that made him appear like a Viking. He was incredibly loyal and a great asset to the company.

"You have known me your whole life Hendrick, I'm sure you know I had nothing to do with dumping waste into the ocean. The person in charge of a decision like that is one of your minions."

"How is it that the owner and CEO of a company had no idea that his own company has been poisoning the ocean?"

"Someone down the line obviously felt it would save the company a lot of money."

Hendrick snorted, "Ya and no one would ever find out that the Arctic Ocean was suddenly polluted? My god they have vessel numbers and everything, it was our guys to be sure, so how do I not know about it?"

"The prosecutors are doing their investigation and so are we. I can guarantee that we will find out who is responsible before anyone else does."

"I'm being prosecuted, Geoffrey! They think I knew about this madness."

"Look you didn't know and they can't prove that you did. You will have your day in court and they will simply have to let it go. They can't pull evidence from thin air so you're safe."

Hendrick went to the side table by the grand picture window. He poured them both a glass of bourbon, handing one to Geoffrey.

"I built this company because I believed in a vision and now our reputation is being smeared. All the while I'm off doing fundraisers and charity events while some asshole is destroying the ocean under my name."

"Hendrick, it's your job to do those things. That's how money is raised and you don't need to be at the company all the time, that's my job, to handle the bullshit. I apologize that this issue slipped through my fingers. I assure you it will be handled, we certainly won't be dealing with such an issue as this in the future."

They clinked glasses before Hendrick took a strong gulp of his.

"What do you suggest for damage control?"

Geoffrey faced the window and looked outside taking a moment to collect his thoughts. He took a sip of bourbon, turning to face Hendrick.

"Africa."

"Excuse me?"

"I've looked into some options and we need huge PR points right now. Not only that but Africa needs people to help build a school and a hospital in one of its most impoverished places."

"And this is going to work?"

"Brilliantly. We are going to give them a ton of money while you are going to fly there and get your hands dirty to show the world what your company really stands for."

"After this mess, it's the least I can do."

"Good, because you leave on Monday."

As Hendrick packed for his trip, he wondered what Africa was going to be like. He had never made a personal trip there and out of all the fundraisers and events none had ever supported Africa, so he had no need to visit there. He made sure to pack light fabrics due to the heat. It might actually be good to get out and work with people again one-on-one.

Lately, it seemed all he did was throw money around. He knew that wasn't always what it was all about. Despite the hard labor he was about to endure, he was looking forward to getting away from the politics of the company. He would also get away from the media.

As he lounged aboard his private jet heading to Africa, he reflected on the life he had led and how much he had in life. He was able to pick up and go on a whim because he didn't have any attachments. He was a 33-year-old man, never married or had children. Hell, he didn't even have a girlfriend. Even though he had, on occasion, taken a girl out for a night in town and then cooked her breakfast in the morning, he rarely ever saw the same person twice. He wasn't opposed to it, and he

didn't view himself as a player, he was just bus[
really bored. It had to take a special kind of lac[
only keep him on his toes, but to provide the kind of
mental and physical stimulation he required to stick
around. He had devoted his whole life to building the
type of empire that would take care of him his entire
life. He had no need to work a day in his life but he
liked to keep busy and he was always in front of the
media. He used to be the poster child for success and
philanthropic acts until his company had been found out
to be polluting the ocean.

He rubbed his hands through his hair in frustration.
He would like to strangle the moron who made that
decision, probably hoping Hendrick would never find
out. Or maybe he thought Hendrick would applaud his
genius. There are many fake philanthropists out there,
but Hendrick wasn't one of them.

"Mr. Cooper, would you like another drink? We are
about to serve your dinner."

"Yes, Amanda, that sounds wonderful. Make it a
little stiffer though this time around."

She smiled at him a little too long and he could tell
just by the look on her face that she would like
something stiff as well. He wouldn't mind taking her
into the back cabin and bending her over, but he had a
strict rule against sleeping with staff. It was all trouble
and he wanted no part of it. He certainly didn't need
more bad press, especially if he happened to anger a
female worker. Although it certainly depended on a
case-by-case situation, he knew that most of the women
that hit on him were looking to marry a handsome

billionaire, and why not, right? What more could a girl ask for?

Although he was going to Africa to help out, he had sent over some luxuries to indulge in such as whiskey, cigars and chocolate. He sent a lot over in order to share; he wasn't greedy. He would be there for a few weeks at least and he wasn't giving up all the things he enjoyed in life.

His dinner was served and he downed the bourbon in one gulp. He delighted in his grilled salmon steak and asparagus. He enjoyed a healthy lifestyle and he happened to enjoy seafood of any kind. It was just as important in his success to keep his body as well as his mind clean and healthy. He decided to take a nap before the jet landed and his new adventure began.

Africa radiated with beauty in the same way that it radiated heat. He was in awe as soon as they arrived at the location in which he would be staying for the time period. He was staying in a cabin with a porch and although it wasn't luxurious, it was perfect for what he would need. He decided to unpack first before finding the man in charge. He noticed his packages had arrived including the wine that Geoffrey had sent in case Hendrick dined with any special guests. There were also pounds of individually wrapped chocolates that would be handed out to the children.

When he finished unpacking, he ventured out to his porch, plopping himself down on a wooden lounge chair. He looked around at all the lush greens of the forest, enamored that such places existed in the world. How lucky was he to be here and how lucky to be part of helping better a village. He noticed he had a hammock and looked forward to lounging in it at night. He had not been in a hammock since he was a kid. Both his parents died when he was 12 and he was raised for the most part by an aunt he was never close to. So again, attachments weren't really his thing.

He got up, grabbed a bottle of water and headed to the site. He wanted to talk to the head honcho and find out what the plan for the day would be. He had arranged, as well as paid for all the supplies that would be needed to build a new school and a hospital that the villagers desperately needed.

He was happy to have worn a hat because the African sun beat down hard. It wasn't overbearing though, and there was none of the humidity that he was used to in the summer months, so the heat there was dry so it didn't feel as hot.

When he arrived on location, the place was bustling with people. Some of the local villagers were around watching the goings on and getting a look at the new visitors. There were many volunteers sorting through supplies and they already had the frame of the school underway. He felt a sudden rush of pride at what he saw and what he was now a part of. The media could kiss his ass if they thought he could ever be involved in poisoning the earth.

"Mr. Cooper, welcome!"

Hendrick turned to find a very red-faced man standing behind him. His pale complexion was clearly not doing well in the sun, causing Hendrick to wonder why the skin wouldn't just tan instead of keeping a perpetual burn. He shook the sweaty palm of the pale fellow.

"It's a pleasure to have you here, sir, the supplies you sent were extremely generous. As you can see, the volunteers have already begun the project."

"Please call me Hendrick, there's no need for formalities here." He smiled warmly as the fella seemed nervous. "And you would be?"

"Oh my apologies, I'm Fred Cambridge, I am head of the project. Many projects actually. I've been here for over a year heading many projects for the corporation your company contacted."

"Perfect, well you're just the man I wanted to see then. What would you like me to help out with? And please I'm willing to help with any dirty work."

Fred chuckled, "Very good then, are you any good with a hammer?"

"I'm actually excellent with a hammer, just show me the way."

Hendrick felt a tugging on his leg and looked down to find a skinny little African girl tugging on the leg of his shorts.

"Well hello there."

The girl smiled up at him with the most beautiful brown eyes he had ever seen.

"Many of the school children wander over during break. Their current school is falling apart and not nearly big enough for the number of children they have.

So from time to time we may have some of the students visiting us."

"Well I look forward to visiting with everyone."

Fred walked Hendrick over to the group and introduced him. Hendrick could tell by the way they looked at him that they knew they had a billionaire amongst them. It was something he was used to at this point; he never quite got treated the same as everyone else. It was no big deal though, people warmed up to him eventually, once they got to know him and realized he wasn't a snobby prick. They got to work immediately and Hendrick felt a soul-cleansing feeling come over him from the hard work.

He hammered into those boards, letting out the pent-up aggression that he felt over the charges against his company. All his anger and pain went into the boards of that school building. By the end of the day they had a full frame completed on the school.

"Wow, it just looks fantastic everyone, good job."

There were plenty of high fives and slaps on the back to go around. Hendrick was sweaty and tired, but he hadn't felt that good in a really long time.

"I would very much like you all to join me at my cabin for dinner tonight. I'm having a fantastic dinner sent over and I want to share it with you all. You deserve it. And if that doesn't excite you I also have booze."

A cheer rang up around him and he laughed. "Ok I will see you in an hour, I'm sure you can find it."

A younger guy, not even 25, approached Hendrick; he thought maybe his name was Adam. "Hey, Hendrick. We have the volunteers at the school to have dinner with as well. Is it okay if I invite them as well?"

"Oh hell ya, of course. The more the merrier."

Adam grinned, "Thanks, man, you're pretty cool."

Hendrick laughed, "Ya I get that sometimes."

Chapter Two

Hendrick had a table set up outside of his cabin, and food had been brought in from the nearest town. Everyone showed up right on time, introductions followed one by one of the volunteers from the school.

There was one woman, he couldn't tell her age, but she had creamy brown skin the color of dark brown sugar with a smile that quite literally lit up the room. He had watched her walk up to his cabin with a few friends, chatting amiably. She stood tall and thin and had the athletic build of a professional dancer. Her eyes were big, round and the color of chestnuts. He could not take his eyes off of her; she was absolutely stunning. Stunning, yet all she wore were cargo shorts and a plain white volunteer t-shirt. She was checking out the food table; it was divine and the volunteers probably hadn't had food like that since they got there.

He made a beeline for her and almost knocked another volunteer over in the process. "I'm sorry," he muttered as he walked by.

Hendrick approached her group as they gathered some food.

"Hello, can I get you guys something to drink?"

She looked up then, meeting his eyes and it was like a gift. He didn't know what the hell was wrong with him because he certainly never went all gooey with any other woman he had been interested in. She smiled very naturally at him and said, "Hi, Mr. Cooper, is it? I'm Jocelyn, I'm one of the AIDS volunteers here."

"Jocelyn, what a beautiful name, and please call me Hendrick."

She blushed at the compliment, pleasing him more.

"Hendrick it is then. Thank you for the invite, we were famished and this looks wonderful."

"You're welcome. I also sent food to the village to help out."

"Oh, well that's very kind of you. I'm sure it's greatly appreciated."

"Well it's nothing for me to do it, so I feel it's my duty."

She stared at him, almost seeing him for the first time. They shook hands and he held hers just a bit too long. So long in fact one of her friends started to giggle.

Composing himself quickly, Hendrick got a drink order from them. He poured Jocelyn and her two friends a glass of wine each and brought it back to them. He didn't want to overstay his welcome with the group. So he handed them their glasses, leaving them to eat. He headed to the table, grabbed a plate full of food and went to sit with Fred. Fred chatted easily with Hendrick as they ate. Hendrick found he didn't have much to say. The food was delicious, chicken and ribs with vegetables and potatoes. Fresh vegetables and fruit came with the food as well and it was a delectable meal.

He found that although it was delicious, he couldn't focus on it much because he kept glancing at Jocelyn. He wanted her, he wanted her more than anything and he was determined to have her. She was easily the most beautiful creature he had even seen; he knew she would be his.

He watched her throughout the night and became more infatuated with her. The best part about it was that she glanced his way on occasion as well, and he could swear that it made him semi-hard every time she did it.

He looked over at Fred who was sipping a bourbon rather happily. "How well do you know the volunteers at the school?"

"Oh quite well. I'm always introduced to new volunteers and they visit our camps regularly."

"What is Jocelyn's story?"

Fred chuckled, "Ah interested in the girl are you? She is beautiful to be sure but she hasn't shown interest in anyone outside of her camp since she's been here. She seems very private."

Hendrick nodded. "She really isn't a girl is she?"

Fred laughed loudly bringing attention to them. Jocelyn met his eyes again, holding them for a beat. Fred carried on, "No, she's 26, I believe, and incredibly smart. I think she is here on a whim to escape her life temporarily. But I guess that's really why we are all here isn't it, Hendrick?"

Hendrick met his gaze and knew that Fred had heard about the trouble with his company. He hoped he didn't think negatively about him; he didn't want anyone to believe the nonsense rumors about him.

"Yes, I'm afraid that's usually the case."

As people started filtering out of the area and returning to their own lodgings, Hendrick boldly went over to Jocelyn and asked if she would stick around and have another drink with him. Her friend giggled again, walking away.

"Sure, I would love that. I can't stay late though. The mornings are far too early for me." She laughed gently and he enjoyed the sound of it.

They walked back up to the porch and Jocelyn sat down on a chair while Hendrick made them a stiff drink. She had been drinking wine all night but he didn't think she would be opposed to liquor. He headed back to the porch and handed her the glass. She didn't miss a beat, taking a sip of her drink. He sat down beside her and they sat in silence for a moment looking out into the lush greens as the sun began to set.

"So tell me Jocelyn, what exactly does your volunteer team do here in regards to the AIDS movement?"

"It's education-based, that's why we are at the schools. We are trying to teach them about the disease and most importantly how to prevent it. It's so rampant here that all we can do is tell them how to avoid it."

"You're pretty young to be doing something like this, aren't you?"

She laughed, "I'm not that young." She stared at him long enough to make the statement hold some power.

"I suppose not, but shouldn't someone of your age be partying and out having some fun."

"Well I certainly did a lot of that when I hit my twenties but I can't say that I'm much for clubbing."

He nodded watching her.

"So what made you come here?"

She turned to face him, "You first. You're quite wealthy, why come down here yourself?"

"Well something happened in my life recently that caused me a bit of trouble. This is my escape, and not only that but it was time I got back into the nitty-gritty. When I was younger I did missions all the time. It's easy to throw money at a situation, but far harder to come down and meet it face-to-face."

"I totally know what you mean. Well not totally," she laughed. "Not the billions."

"So, your turn."

"I came down because my life was too easy and I felt guilty." She looked into her hands unable to meet his gaze any longer.

"Hmmm. I think you're going to have to explain that one."

She looked at him wistfully and took a deep breath. "Well I don't have a terrible back story. And you would be surprised how many people look at me and expect me to have an incredible journey attached to my success and I don't."

"What kind of story should you have?"

"I'm not explaining myself very well here, am I?"

He chuckled, "No worries, please explain."

"Well I'm not from the projects. My family is normal and educated. There are no drunks or crime in our family. I led a normal life and I ended up going to University for fashion and once I graduated, my father lent me the money to start my own design business. Although I'm not rich and famous yet, my company does turn a decent profit."

"That's something to be proud of, Jocelyn. So how does the guilt fit into this?"

"You are so easy to talk to, I hadn't expected that." They smiled at each other and he couldn't have felt happier that he caused her comfort.

"Hold that thought, while I grab us another drink." Hendrick quickly went in and poured them a short drink. It was getting late and he didn't want her to feel hung-over in the morning. He returned, handing her the glass.

"Please tell me why you feel guilty about your success."

"Well I met a girl in University who did have a tragic upbringing and she fought to get through school and she did her thesis paper on the history of the African-Americans and so on."

She paused and he waited her out. He sipped his drink, completely mesmerized by this girl.

"My friend made me feel guilty I guess. We still remained close after University and she went into politics and I went into fashion. One day she showed me this video about things going on in the world. She implored me to start helping out and suddenly I looked at my life seeing all that I had. I just felt it, ya know? Felt that I too needed to give back because I had been so lucky. So I put my sister in-charge of my company temporarily and I came here. I plan on being here for a month and I'm almost done, so I'm doing the best that I can with the time I have."

"Wow, I don't even know you Jocelyn and I'm incredibly proud of you. Your parents must have been thrilled."

She laughed, "Actually they weren't. They felt they had worked really hard to give me a better life, a different life than they had growing up. They wanted me to reap the benefits of it, not immerse myself into the very life they had wanted me to avoid."

"They will come around. Parents always want the best for their kids and it's usually what they want for themselves more. You did something great, it's only temporary and then you will be back making dresses in no time."

"Thank you, Hendrick, I appreciate you saying that."

"Oh, you know I'm wise beyond my years," he joked trying to make light of their talk.

"Oh you can't be that much older than me."

"I'm a bit, I'll be turning 34 in six months. I have lots of experience."

"Experience in what?" she whispered. And it was the way she whispered that caught him off guard. It was almost like she was breathless.

He couldn't find any words to answer her and he felt like he was losing a handle on things.

"I like you, Hendrick, I feel like you understand me."

"I like you too, Jocelyn, a little too much for my own good."

"Well we can't be good all the time, can we?"

He just stared at her. Her brown eyes bore into his. He wanted to ravish her right then but he didn't know if he should make a move. They had just met and he didn't want to start something he couldn't finish. They would be working together now and he didn't want to make things worse. However, there was the problem of how he could only think of sliding inside her and seeing what she felt like wrapped around him.

She got up then and made the decision for him. She bore her mouth onto his and the fire that lit between them was intense. She gasped inside his mouth and his loins burned for her. His hands went into her hair, pulling her closer to him. He kissed her deeply finding her tongue and sucking on it gently. She moaned and the sounds she made caused him to go rock hard. Oh yes, he would have her tonight. He needed to hear her moan all night long.

He stood up then and pulled her body to his. He kissed down to her chin and trailed kisses down her neck sucking on her. Her hands found the bulge in his shorts, rubbing him hard causing a friction that drove him insane. The knowledge that she was eager for his cock drove him half mad. He picked her up, carrying her into the cabin and laid her out on his bed. He pulled off her t-shirt and unclasped her bra. Her breasts dropped deliciously from the bra and he bent down to suck on her dark nipples. She gave a guttural moan and he sucked even harder. She pushed him away, tearing off her shorts and he glimpsed a pair of white lace panties before she slid them to the floor.

He dropped to the floor in front of her, spreading her legs as she leaned back. Her pussy was so pink it made him crazy. She was already wet and he slid a finger inside her, feeling her drip down his finger. She moaned his name and it was just about the best sound he had ever heard. He leaned in and sucked her clit forcing her to thrash beneath him. He sucked her good while fucking her with his finger. She came all over his finger and he pulled out.

"Please, Hendrick, I want you inside me."

He never wanted a lady to beg; he would give her exactly what she wanted. He pulled her up and turned her over. She gasped in excitement as she bent over for him, her tight round bottom in his face. He bent down and kissed her bottom, moving in real close to her. He was rock hard and he couldn't wait to plunge inside her pink little pussy. Her tight bottom drove him insane and he drove deep inside her causing her to moan loudly. She was tight and wet and he really had to control himself or he would lose himself completely inside her.

"Hendrick, I need it."

Her ass looked glorious right before him as he plunged deeper inside and moved within her. She called out to him loudly and he briefly wondered if there was anyone within earshot. He could have cared less however; let the whole village hear. He was fucking an amazing woman and he wouldn't stop for anything.

She came against his cock and he continued to rock inside her until he spilled into her as well. He leaned down on top of her back, breathing heavily into her hair.

"Oh Jocelyn, that was incredible."

"You bet your ass it was," and she giggled underneath him. He rolled off of her and lay down on the bed. She lay beside him and they were silent thinking about what had just happened between them. She rolled into his chest and nuzzled into it. He wrapped his hands around her and kissed her on the top of the head.

"Yes that definitely was amazing." They fell asleep tangled up in each other's arms.

Chapter Three

When Hendrick awoke that morning, he felt glorious. He had slept like the dead and despite the hard labor of the day before, he awoke completely rested, ready to start the day. He rolled over to kiss Jocelyn good morning and realized he was in the bed alone. She must have woken before him, dressed and left while he slept. He hadn't even heard her leave. He suddenly worried that she might be upset.

He washed up in the basin left out for him and dressed quickly. He was determined to talk to Jocelyn before he began the work for the day. But when he arrived at the old school she was nowhere to be found. He asked her friends if they had seen her and although they both had a mischievous glint in their eyes, they claimed that neither had seen her that morning. He was starting to run late so he headed to his camp, knowing he would have to try to meet up with her later.

The sun beat down heavy on them that day and although they accomplished a lot by lunch, he was utterly exhausted from the heat. He would have given anything for a cold shower at that point.

Instead of heading with the crowd to find lunch, he grabbed a bottle of water and headed to the school. He had not been able to stop thinking about Jocelyn all morning. It was very unlike him; usually he could forget a girl he slept with by lunch. Jocelyn was different however; she intrigued him. He saw her when he entered the school yard, she was with the children playing outside.

He walked right up to her and she smiled when she saw him. "Hendrick, I didn't expect you, welcome to the school."

She didn't appear uncomfortable or awkward at all.

"Can we talk?"

Surprise crossed her face and she looked around at the children. "Why don't you guys go back inside so we can begin the lesson?"

"Take these with you." He handed the children a handful of chocolates. They ran inside excitedly ripping them open as they ran.

Jocelyn laughed as they ran away. "Well that sure worked."

He watched her, "You left this morning."

"Yes. Did that bother you?"

"No. I just wanted to make sure you weren't upset about what happened last night."

"How could I be upset, you made me feel quite good."

She had a glint in her eye that made him envision a teacher's desk and her bent over it.

"Well good, I'm glad. I don't want you to be."

"I wasn't sure if it would have been weird for you to wake up beside me, so I got up. I needed to get ready for work anyways."

"I would like the chance to wake up beside you if you allow me to."

"Oh my, Hendrick, what are you suggesting?"

"I'm suggesting you allow me to touch your body anytime I want to."

She gasped. But she didn't say no.

A week passed and Jocelyn was over every night. He filled her with his cock every night. She was a drug to him and he could not get enough of her. The second night they were together, he put his cock in her mouth and she did things to it that made him see heaven early. All he did was fuck her in every position he could imagine; he needed to have her over and over again. He was insatiable when he was around her. He couldn't even have a peaceful dinner with her without needing his dessert first; only then could they sit and enjoy a meal.

New volunteers had arrived and the school was almost finished. They had a rather large team at this point, so work finished quickly. Next they would begin the hospital and then who knows? Geoffrey was showing up that day to give him an update on the company. He didn't have his phone with him; it would have been far too distracting so he had left it at home. So that meant Geoffrey travelling to Africa to bring Hendrick any news.

When Geoffrey arrived, Hendrick was having lunch with Jocelyn at her camp. It took Geoffrey awhile to find Hendrick and he was drenched in sweat when he finally did.

"Holy it's hot here."

Hendrick laughed, "Well you get used to it."

Hendrick introduced Geoffrey to Jocelyn and he could tell that Geoffrey liked her immediately.

"I have an update for you on the issue, if we could talk in private."

"Ya let's do that." He looked at Jocelyn and she had a puzzled look on her face.

"I will see you later, okay?"

She nodded, not saying a word. Hendrick thought her behavior was a little weird, but he quickly forgot it when he walked away with Geoffrey.

"So what's the word, my good man?"

"You look really good, Hendrick, nice and relaxed, good for you."

"Thanks to you. This was a great idea, I needed to get away from all the stress of being accused of poisoning the ocean."

"I know, believe me we are going to walk away from this."

"Good, so what's the word?"

"You need to be finished here in a few weeks whether the hospital is complete or not because you are to appear in front of the court for the criminal charges brought against you."

"I'm not going to jail because the Arctic Ocean was poisoned."

"You aren't, Hendrick, it's all going to go away, swept under the rug and everyone will be back to thinking you are as amazing as always."

"Awesome, that's what I like to hear."

They continued walking to the camp so that Hendrick could show him the progress of the project but neither of them had noticed the person walking behind them the whole time.

Chapter Four

When Jocelyn didn't show up at his cabin for dinner that night, Hendrick grew worried and went out to look for her. He didn't have to look far, however, as she had never left her own camp the whole night. He found her out on the grass of her own cabin. She didn't even look up at him as he approached.

"Hey, what happened to you tonight? I thought you were coming over?"

"Well I guess you thought wrong, Hendrick."

Shocked, he didn't know how to respond, she sounded so cold.

"Is something wrong? Have I done something to upset you?"

She finally looked up at him and just glared. He couldn't have been more confused at that moment. He didn't know what to say to her, so he said nothing. Girls usually spoke again anyways; they were always so inclined to make sure their word was spoken and no man would be getting the upper hand on them.

She was still staring at him and he could swear she bore a hole right through him.

"You poisoned that ocean. You came down here and you're nothing but a fake."

He was so taken aback that he didn't know how to respond, which made him look completely guilty.

"Why would you say that to me?"

"I heard you and your friend talking today. You guys were so immersed in your evil that you didn't even notice I was right behind you."

"No, Jocelyn, you don't understand. I mean yes what you heard was correct, but I had nothing to do with it."

"Oh well how convenient for you. It's not like we haven't heard that story before. Something dirty goes on in a company and the owner just has no idea, right?"

"I assure you, Jocelyn, I had no idea, I'm rarely even at the company anymore."

"That doesn't mean you don't know what's going on there. Like who really has no idea what their own company is doing in regards to waste management?"

He couldn't even believe what he was hearing. He had said the very same thing before heading to Africa. And now Jocelyn didn't believe a word he said.

"I know it sounds crazy, but it's true. Even Geoffrey had no idea. I am going to court but it doesn't mean I did it. I'm defending myself, I had no idea that this was something that was going on at my company and the prosecutor can't prove otherwise."

"It's completely disgusting what happened and I just have a hard time believing you had nothing to do with it."

"Please, Jocelyn. I have spent my whole life trying to do right by people. You know me, really you already know me so well. I would never do something so careless and stupid, I'm trying to better the world, not ruin it."

"Are you here to run away from the press?"

"No, the complete opposite actually. I want them to see who I really am and then judge my character. I've only been here a week and I am so much happier than I have been in years."

She looked at him deep in the eyes and seemingly searched for answers. He didn't know what he could do that would make her believe him. He felt like she should already know his character.

"Please come back to my cabin with me. Being near you is driving me crazy."

"Please don't lie to me."

"I would never. I'm telling you the truth, please believe me."

She leaned into him and kissed him roughly. It excited him and he started undressing her right then. He knew she shared a cabin with the two other girls from the school but he didn't care.

"Hendrick, we can't."

"Shhh, we'll be quiet, I'm not waiting."

They quickly undressed each other and he lay her down in the grass, spreading her legs wide. He liked looking at her pink pussy, it drove him insane with lust.

Her opening was always wet and ready for him. He slid a finger inside her and rocked her gently. She was holding back her cries. He got his finger very wet from her pussy and slowly inserted it into her bum being careful that he was gentle. She couldn't hold back; she cried out in pleasure and he inserted his finger repeatedly. He loved looking at her in the throes of passion.

He took his finger out and climbed on top of her, pushing his cock inside. He pumped inside her hard and she fought back the moans she so desperately wanted to scream out. He had her alright and he made her come over and over again as he fucked her with an intensity she would not soon forget. He finally spilled into her and they lay together in the grass, spent. He rolled over to her and kissed her deeply on the mouth.

"You have completely bewitched me, Jocelyn, whatever am I going to do with you?"

"Anything you want, Hendrick, anything you want."

He had returned that night to his own bed though he wished that she had went with him. He could still remember the feeling of being inside her and he wanted to do it all over again before he went to bed. He would have to wait another evening however. He fell asleep as soon as his head hit the pillow.

When the sun hit his eyes that morning he opened them to find Jocelyn already there with two cups of coffee in her hands. He rubbed at his eyes sure that it was a dream.

"What are you doing here? Why didn't you just come back with me last night?"

"I was torn, I'm sorry. I have something to tell you."

"What is it?"

"I'm leaving today."

He sat right up in bed and said, "What?"

"I'm sorry, I should have told you sooner but I didn't want to make a big thing of it. I just wanted to enjoy my time with you and then go. My time serving here is over. I've already been gone a month and my sister needs me to take my company off her hands. I have to go."

"I can't believe you're going. What am I going to do here without you?"

She laughed, "Work, I suppose. I really enjoyed our time together Hendrick but I need to get back to my life and move on. I hope you understand."

He didn't of course, but he refused to let her see that he was devastated. There was nothing he could do about her sudden departure so it was best he let her go and figure out a way to deal with it later.

"Sure. I wish you well with your company."

A sad look came over her and she leaned in to kiss him.

"Take care, Hendrick."

And with that he watched her walk out of his cabin and into the lush green of the forest around them.

-To be continued in Book 2-

Book Two – Love Belated

Chapter One

JOCELYN WAS rushing around like a chicken with her head cut off. To say she was stressed out would be an understatement. She hurried into the cafe around the corner from her studio and grabbed coffee as well as the most delicious donuts for her whole team. She put in her order and tried with all her might to be patient while it was made. She had a huge deadline due that day to provide sketches for a well-known female rock star for an upcoming awards show and she needed everything to go fabulously. She needed this job to bring her career to the next level.

She had been working like a well-trained poodle since she came back from Africa six months prior. She wanted to start making things happen in her life just as she had always imagined. Or maybe it had a lot to do with the man she had left in Africa. She had not spoken to Hendrick since she left and she knew it was the best thing. The man was trouble. It had been a short little fling that she was determined to keep in her past and that was that. She had to question her drive lately and how much that had to do with the fact that she was trying to forget feelings that she had begun to develop with Hendrick. What a fool. What, you fell in love after a few weeks? She wasn't about to believe that and she certainly wasn't going to tie herself pathetically to a man that had never had a serious relationship in his entire life. No thank you.

So she dove into her work with great gusto in the hopes that she could forget the way in which he ignited her body every time he touched her. It had been good for her though; the work she had put into her company in the past six months had grown it significantly. Now she had a team behind her that worked with her in creating her designs. She used to do all the sewing herself and getting everything ready for shows, and now she was able to delegate those tasks to someone else. It was the most empowering and liberating feeling to be in her position. But it also meant she stood in a coffee line stressed to the nines waiting for a beverage. Man, if she could just get this songstress to wear her designs she would be laughing. The girl could virtually wear garbage bags and people went nuts, so having her wear her own designs would definitely benefit her greatly.

Coffee trays in hand she headed for the door. Her team deserved frequent coffee fixes, they had worked so hard, so it was the least she could do for them. Plus in general, she just enjoyed making people happy. When she stepped out into the sun and headed towards her studio she stopped abruptly in the middle of the sidewalk. Screw it, she thought, I'm taking a moment. She stood there on the sidewalk and just pointed her face toward the sky and took a deep relaxing breath. She loved her life and all the great things she had. She was blessed in so many ways and she had no reason to be stressed. With so many people dying in the world, her designs were hardly anything to worry about. And what's more, she was genuinely happy and delighted for her future.

She walked the rest of the way to her office with a new lightness of foot. When she walked into the open concept room, one of her girls ran over and grabbed one of the trays out of her hands.

"Oh thank you. I was so worried I was going to spill coffee and donuts on my way over here."

The girl's name was Samantha and she was Jocelyn's right hand lady. Samantha laughed as she helped Jocelyn with passing out the coffee.

"You got a package today, it looks sort of luxurious."

Jocelyn laughed, "Really? Maybe little miss rock star is trying to bribe my designs in early."

"You don't know who it's from?"

"I couldn't even imagine."

Samantha followed Jocelyn over to her desk and they both stared down at the box. It certainly was an expensively wrapped package and staring at it puzzled Jocelyn further.

"I don't know Jose, it sort of looks romantic."

"Romantic?" Jocelyn laughed and with that she quickly opened the package to find a stunning red dress inside with a necklace that screamed big dollars.

"Oh my god."

"There's a letter, open it!" Samantha practically yelled.

"Okay, okay, I will."

She picked up the letter and turned it over; there was no name or address on it. She opened it and there in simple words was a message to meet at Le Amore, the fanciest restaurant in town. She was to wear the elegant items in the box.

"Who on earth...?"

"It has to be Tim," Samantha squealed.

Jocelyn grew warm all over with the sound of his name. "Really? You think so?"

"Sure he sent you all those flowers last week, of course it's him. He's quite smitten with you."

"I don't know, this is a pretty big jump from flowers."

"Not really, plus he can obviously afford it."

Jocelyn stared hard at the letter willing it to tell her who sent it.

"Should I go?"

"Are you mad? Of course you should go. Some romantic guy sends you this and you're thinking of not going?"

"What if it's Jack the Ripper waiting at the table."

"What are you talking about?"

"Well with all the publicity lately, really this could be anyone."

"You are over-thinking this, you met a great guy last week, it's him for sure. You guys have been talking non-stop since then."

"Maybe you're right."

Samantha left Jocelyn to her own thoughts and returned to her work, coffee in hand. Jocelyn sat down at her desk and read the note again while fingering the beautiful fabric. She knew fabric and this was expensive and she couldn't even guess the amount spent on the necklace. Samantha was right; it was a luxurious package.

Tim came to mind then and she smiled. Would he really have done this? It seemed awful soon for him to be surprising her with such things, but they had hit it off wonderfully so maybe it was him.

She had met Tim just over a week ago at an AIDS benefit. She had been trying to get more involved since she left Africa and she had made a donation of one of her designs to help out. Tim had been seated at her table, on purpose she believed. He was older than her of course and owned one of the major football teams; he was quite successful for a man of his age. Skin the same shade as her own, and a body that was hard all over. She had been dreaming about that body ever since they met.

They had enjoyed a great night together at the benefit and a friend of hers had mentioned later on in the night that he had requested to sit at her table. She couldn't have been more surprised. They hadn't known each other prior, so what had caused him to want to spend time with her? In the end she had been thankful for his company because she couldn't have imagined the night being better without him. At the end of the night he had asked her to dinner the next night and she accepted without another thought. After a night of lobsters and great conversation, she went home wondering if she had met her match. He was smart, successful and sexy as all hell. And although she dreamed about his body constantly, they had not slept together yet.

Jocelyn smiled again deciding that she was going to go meet her mystery man.

<<<>>>

Drinking a glass of wine as she got ready for her dinner date, Jocelyn finally felt relaxed. She got the sketches sent over an hour ahead of schedule and all became well with the world once again. She couldn't wait to get the word on the sketches and wondered how long it would take to get word back on them.

She checked herself in the mirror, the dress fitting like a glove. How had Tim guessed her size so easily without having slept with her? He wouldn't have even had a chance to check out her clothing tags. She gently put the necklace on, feeling its heaviness against her chest. She gasped when she saw the final product of herself. She looked like a movie star. She giggled excitedly, anxious to get to the restaurant to see the look on Tim's face when he saw her in the dress. She left her panties at home, thinking she might give Tim a night he would never forget.

She cabbed it to the restaurant not wanting to have to worry about driving buzzed. She stepped into the gloriously expensive restaurant and waited to be seated.

You usually had to wait months to get a reservation there but here she was. Tim must have some serious connections.

She was seated on the terrace to the restaurant, one of the best seats in the restaurant. The view was just breathtaking. She was mesmerized by it when she noticed her date approaching the table.

Her mouth dropped open rather inelegantly and she gaped in surprise as Hendrick approached the table with an ear-to-ear grin. The last time she had seen him was that last morning in Africa. She was startled to find that her heart raced at the sight of him and her temperature rose significantly.

Oh god, what's wrong with me? She was suddenly embarrassed to find her thoughts drifting to a more sexual nature when she saw him smile.

"Well hello Jocelyn, you look absolutely radiant."

"Hendrick, what are you doing here?"

"Should I be alarmed that I'm not the man you were expecting?"

She chose not to answer him and instead just smiled.

"The city may be a big one darling but I can still find you."

"Well this is certainly one way of doing it," she laughed.

He sat down and she instantly felt guilty. She had expected Tim and here sat a man from her past. How would Tim feel if he knew she was here with Hendrick? Her thoughts became torn as she really liked Tim. Liked him so much in fact that she had been having thoughts that included white lace and diamonds. Tim was the perfect guy to marry and start a family with; he would make her incredibly happy. But she had intense chemistry with Hendrick and although she knew there was potential for happiness with Hendrick, she could never truly feel confident that he would be there tomorrow when she needed him.

"So how have you been?" He smiled warmly at her and it lit her up inside.

Jocelyn blushed, "I've been great, I'm actually waiting on a call to see if a celeb is going to use my design."

"Wow, congratulations Jocelyn, though I'm not surprised at all."

She beamed at him from across the table and felt completely at ease with him. They ordered some champagne in celebration of her new potential clients. Dinner just flew by and they talked through the whole dinner unable to stop. It was like they had been without oxygen this whole time and finally found it again. They had talked about her growing business and what he had achieved in Africa. She could tell just by the way he talked that the experience changed him, and for the better. He explained to her what was going on in his case, the fact that it was coming up. He seemed anxious to get it over with and she knew it brought him unnecessary stress.

Just then her phone rang and thinking it was her design team, she told Hendrick she needed to check. She was surprised to see Tim's name flashing on the screen and she immediately sent the call to voicemail. There was no point in trying to talk to him now; that was something she would have to deal with tomorrow. She looked up to see a curious expression on Hendrick's face.

"Who was it?" He had a territorial glint in his eyes that she actually found rather sexy.

"That's none of your business."

Her phone rang again causing her to flush with embarrassment. They both laughed.

"Popular girl tonight."

"I'm sorry."

"No, please, take your time."

She dug her phone out quickly and saw that it was Samantha calling. She answered it promptly and heard the excited chatter of Samantha ringing through the phone.

"Samantha slow down, I can barely understand you."

There was a long pause and Jocelyn's face registered shock.

"Are you serious? Oh wow! I can't believe it, or maybe I can." She started laughing. She quickly said goodbye to Samantha and put her phone away.

"What was that all about?"

Unable to wipe the grin off of her face, Jocelyn took a deep breath trying to calm her heart from racing so much.

"It was my assistant. I got my first celebrity client. My god she just had my sketches for a matter of hours and she already wants me."

Hendrick got up from his chair to go to her. She stood up to accept his hug. "I'm so happy for you Jocelyn." She felt a loss of control when their bodies touched, her mind weakening against the resolve against him. They parted and he looked into her eyes intensely. He kissed her then, right in the middle of Le Amore. She kissed him back.

When they parted he said, "I have a room upstairs, would you like to come up for a bit?"

She nodded unable to speak.

Chapter Two

They entered the penthouse suite without saying a word. As soon as the door closed, Hendrick wrapped his arms around Jocelyn picking her up. He carried her to the master suite, laying her down on the bed.

Her mind was racing as she watched him undress before her. She didn't know if this was the right thing to do and she wondered about her growing feelings for Tim. She was suddenly torn between two men. Her thoughts suddenly shut down when he dropped his underwear. His hard cock stood up, ready for her. She stood up to take off her dress but Hendrick stopped her.

"I want to fuck you with that dress on."

She smiled and crushed his mouth with a kiss searching out his tongue, sucking on it. He moaned and the sound thrilled her. His hands found her bottom and squeezed. She kissed his jawline, nipping at his throat. Her hands found his cock as she played with his balls before bending down. She got down on her knees taking his cock in her mouth.

He let out a long moan his hands lost in her hair. She sucked hard while massaging his balls. His cock hit the back of her throat and he called out her name. She moved in rhythm over his cock, starting off slow then picking up the pace.

"God, Jocelyn that feels incredible."

She continued to suck him twirling her tongue around his tip.

"Darling, I need to be inside you."

She slid him out of her mouth gently as he helped her back up. There was a fire in his eyes and she knew she was in for a night to remember. She lay back down onto the bed, spreading her legs for him. He loved the look of her pussy and he climbed on top of her, lifting her dress to take a look. He was pleased to see no panties and he slid a finger inside. He finger fucked her fast, enjoying the look of ecstasy that came over her face.

"Hendrick come inside me, please. I want you so badly."

Resting her feet on his shoulders he plunged deep inside her. She gasped as the full length of him went inside her, pumping in and out. She called out his name which drove him mad.

"Your pussy feels amazing Jocelyn, I can't get enough of you."

She could barely think as waves of pleasure washed over her continuously. She had lost all ability to think and reason. She only saw him, felt him and she had never felt so complete. She felt a tension build up inside of her and she came on his cock, releasing an orgasm so strong it rocked her body. He came soon after and fell exhausted onto her chest. She kissed his head gently pulling her fingers through his hair. She felt so satisfied she could have fallen asleep right then and there.

Her eyes snapped open. No she was not going to spend the night, absolutely not.

He rolled over and lay on his back, eyes closed breathing deeply. She lay on her side and watched him. He was a handsome man, complicated but handsome.

"Come with me to Greece for a few days."

She laughed loudly. "Umm... no. I have a life here I can't just pick up and go."

"You just got a great client, celebrate, you can take a few days off."

"I have to start work on her dress."

"Start her dress on Monday."

"Hendrick, I can't."

It was their last day in Greece and Jocelyn still couldn't believe she had let Hendrick talk her into going. She had to lie to her staff because she didn't want anyone to know she was taking off with another guy when they knew Tim was around. She had called Tim the next day and explained she would be out of town for a few days, but she would talk to him when she returned. She needed to make a decision after all; she couldn't keep carrying on like this.

Hendrick already had the private jet so they left for Greece immediately, and having never been there it was everything she had hoped it would be. The first day however, they hadn't left the room once, the result being she was sore the entire next day because of it. They had done very little sightseeing, not that she cared; it was such a rushed trip that all she wanted to do was lounge on the beach and soak up some sun.

It had been a great trip so far and she actually enjoyed the shopping the most. There were some incredible fabrics there that she snapped up for the studio. Hendrick spoiled her rotten with clothing and shoes. Being a billionaire must be something to get used to.

Now they were lounging by their private pool sipping margaritas and she couldn't have been happier. Hendrick left to call in room service so she decided to check to see if she had any messages. For obvious reasons she hadn't been checking her messages often and she noticed two text messages that had come in from Tim. One was wishing her well on her trip and the next was a question about how her trip was going. She sent a quick text back to him asking if he wanted to grab dinner tomorrow night when she arrived back in town, because she felt they needed to talk.

She turned around as Hendrick walked back out to the balcony. He looked annoyed to find her on the phone. "I ordered in room service so we can relax tonight and catch an early flight in the jet tomorrow."

"Sounds great."

"Is work bugging you?"

She hesitated, "They just want me back, that's all."

He stared at her and she wasn't sure if he believed her. She was surprised when he leaned in to kiss her. He claimed her tongue and roughly squeezed her breasts. She moaned and started rubbing his cock through his shorts. They had taken a day off sex because she had been so sore but she was ready to take him in again.

Their hands were everywhere while their tongues mingled and she felt herself grow wet with yearning. She wanted him inside her immediately.

"Fuck me Hendrick, right now."

She peeled off her bikini top and bottom and ran to the pool and jumped in. She giggled as she reached the surface and he was just plunging in after her. She swam to the shallow end and waited by the edge of the pool. He quickly found her, pushing her up against the wall. His mouth was on hers eagerly and she moaned loudly aching all over her body. She wrapped her legs around his waist and he entered her hard, pumping into her fast. Her body exploded with pleasure and she wrapped her legs around him tighter. He bit into her neck causing her to cry out with pleasure.

"Oh Hendrick, your cock feels so good."

"You're all mine baby."

"Oh it feels so good."

He plunged inside her deep until she came, arching her back into the edge of the pool. He continued to pump inside her harder still until he came.

Exhausted she leaned into his neck and hugged him with her arms. He made her feel incredible; their chemistry just made their sex life so much better.

He pulled apart from her and said, "Let's go see if the food is here." His grin made her laugh and she climbed out of the pool with him. As she towelled herself dry she watched as he went back into the room to check on the room service. She felt so satisfied she could have fallen asleep right then and there.

She quickly checked her phone noticing Tim had messaged her back. She felt guilty once again knowing what she had just done, but in truth she wasn't even dating Tim and they hadn't even slept together. She was just trying to make the best decision possible for herself. His message indicated that he would pick her up at her apartment the next evening. That pleased her so she put her phone away and headed back inside.

Chapter Three

Dinner had been delicious and they lay in the bed talking about the things that were happening for both of them in the next few months. He had ordered up champagne and strawberries and she was enjoying them as they talked. They laughed so easily together she couldn't believe how lucky she was for finding all these great men in her life. She had never had a bad guy in her life and she had no intention of starting with that kind of choice. She just wanted to be happy and fall in love with a great guy. Wasn't that what every girl wanted?

They lay side by side and she thought it was as good a time to talk about the future with him.

"So Hendrick, where do you see this going?"

"What do you mean?"

She sat up laughing, "I mean where do you see this going," she said motioning between the two of them.

"Are we seriously having 'the talk'?"

She was a little put off by his behavior. So in the best firm voice she could muster she said, "Yes Hendrick."

He was silent for a bit and then said, "I thought we were just having fun."

It felt like a weight had dropped in her stomach. "Fun? You're joking right?"

"I don't mean it like that Jocelyn."

"Then how do you mean it?"

He sighed. "I'm not ready for a girlfriend. I have a lot going on right now with the court case and you have things going on too. I enjoy spending time with you but I don't see the need to rush anything right now."

She did not like his answer at all. In fact she hated it. She just stared at him. He could tell that he had upset her. "Look, I'm not saying I don't want something more with you, I just want to take it really slow. I've never been in anything long term and it's a little bit of a shock to the system."

She couldn't at all believe what she was hearing. She felt like slapping him.

"Okay, I think we are on two very different pages here. And had I known that, I wouldn't have flown to Greece with you."

"What are you talking about Jocelyn, what were you expecting, a marriage proposal?"

His words felt like a slap.

"No Hendrick I wasn't looking for a proposal, I was just looking to matter."

She had successfully rendered him silent.

"You can afford another room I'm sure. I would prefer to sleep elsewhere tonight."

"You're not serious."

"Oh but I am."

"You are overreacting."

"Do me a favor Hendrick, don't tell me how I'm feeling. I think things are officially done between us. Please arrange for another room or I will do it myself."

He got up and called to the front desk while she dressed quickly. She gathered together everything she would need for the night.

"I'm sorry Hendrick, I just think we want different things in our lives."

He didn't bother to say anything; she could see he was seething at the thought of her sleeping in another bed.

"I will see you in the lobby in the morning to return home."

It wasn't long before the room service attendant arrived at their room and escorted her to another one. She didn't sleep at all that night.

Once back at her apartment Jocelyn started unpacking. She had a busy night ahead of her and she wanted to be settled before heading out for the night. She was to have dinner with Tim and originally she had planned on letting him down easy. She had believed she was on the road to a future with Hendrick but things hadn't turned out the way she planned. Honestly, who does such a grand gesture as he had just for a little fun? But maybe that's what billionaires did since money was no object after all.

She had been very upset to sleep apart from Hendrick; the whole experience had been upsetting, she couldn't even understand it. The jet ride home had been really long and extremely awkward since neither of them spoke the entire ride home. She could tell he had a lot on his mind, but he never once spoke to her about it. They had landed and he had sent for two separate limos, and that had been the last she had spoken to him.

Her mind was a mess but she wasn't going to cancel on Tim, not after how she had treated him lately. There would be no sex between them however; her mind was too muddled for that.

She quickly got dressed and met Tim down in her lobby.

<<<>>>

The next two months flew by and Jocelyn was in a whirlwind of happiness. She couldn't have asked for anything else in life, it was all just pure bliss. After the night that she returned from Greece she had rarely left Tim's side. They had begun a romance that couldn't have gone better for her. She was completely falling so hard for Tim; he was such an incredible man and knowing that he would do anything for her was exactly part of why she loved him so much.

So much had happened over the course of two months: her celebrity clientele had multiplied due to her one client who not only wore her design to the music awards but started to wear her casual styles all over town. She had seen one of her sundresses in a magazine in Europe and she almost died. She and Tim had spent every waking moment together and she just adored him. They had gone on a few day trips to The Hamptons to visit friends of his and she had actually met his parents. She was just... well happy.

She had decided to not tell him anything about Hendrick. It turned out things between them had just been a fling. At no point had he even called to apologize. Just nothing in months. She didn't see any reason to worry Tim unnecessarily. More than that though she didn't want to hurt him for anything. She had been the one foolish enough to believe there had been something between her and Hendrick so there was no need for Tim to get hurt because she was a fool.

She was putting finishing touches on her wardrobe when Tim walked through the door of her apartment. She had considered asking him to move in with her, but after her experience with Hendrick she felt it was too soon.

"My god Jose, you look gorgeous. How on earth did I get so lucky?"

She went to him and kissed him on the mouth. "I'm the lucky one."

"We're both lucky. Are you ready to go my love?"

They headed out the door to go to dinner. He was taking her to an Italian bistro and she couldn't be more excited to eat a ton of pasta. Later they were going to spend the night at his place.

They ordered and chatted casually about the day they each had. She told him about the design she had seen in Europe and he looked at her with pride.

"I wasn't going to do this tonight, I actually wasn't sure when I was going to. Just whenever it felt right I guess."

"What's that baby?"

He pulled out a ring box from Tiffany & Co. and slid it across the table. She stared at it stunned.

"What's in there?"

He laughed, "Well open it and find out silly."

She did just that and gasped when she saw a two-karat princess cut diamond solitaire in a platinum band.

"I fell for you the moment I laid eyes on you, Jocelyn. Please do me the honor of being my wife."

It had been everything that she had wanted. She was dismayed however when Hendrick flashed into her mind at that moment. Shaking her head she wanted to erase him from her mind.

"You're not saying no I hope," Tim laughed nervously.

She looked up at him and smiled. "I'm saying yes."

<<◇>>

They hurried to his place after that and as soon as the door closed they started tearing their clothes off. Their mouths joined in lust, intensity and hope for their future. His mouth was on her breasts sucking at her hard nipples and her body arched into his as he did it. She ached between her legs and willed for him to enter her.

"Baby, please, do it now."

"I love when you talk like that."

She was kissing him again and the feeling of his tongue in her mouth made her instantly wet. His hard body was pressed against hers. He lifted her up into his arms and her legs circled his waist. He impaled her on his cock and she moaned loudly.

"Oh Tim, that's so good."

"That's all for you baby."

"Give it to me Tim, oh please. Really good."

He must have had insane upper body strength to keep her in his arms to fuck her properly. He did an amazing job because she was spent and wrapped around his neck while still inside her.

"I love you Jose," he whispered.

"I love you too Tim," she whispered back.

Chapter Four

That night they lay in bed together eating ice cream and watching the late night news. It was something they grew fond of doing together before they turned in for the night. She was surprised to see Hendrick on TV. They were announcing his court case had come to a close and he had been acquitted of all the charges against him. She almost jumped on the bed to celebrate but kept herself composed. She was truly happy for Hendrick, now hopefully he could build up the company in the way he wanted to.

Tim snorted, "Man, what a douchebag that guy is. I wonder how much it cost him to buy himself out of that one."

"What?" Jocelyn was genuinely shocked at what she was hearing.

"Oh ya, that guy is total slime. He knew exactly what was going on there. How could he not?"

"Tim you don't even know him. Those are pretty harsh words for someone you don't even know."

He looked at her strangely. "Babe, why are you getting so defensive? What do you care what my opinion of the guy is?"

Guilt filled her heart and she felt stupid. Why was she arguing with him over a man who treated her like a fling and who she had originally planned on dropping Tim for. She would have lost everything.

"Jocelyn, what is it?"

"I know him, I know Hendrick."

"What? How?"

"I met him on the AIDS mission actually."

"Oh my god. I heard about him going off to save face. Why didn't I connect the two before?"

"There's more. We sort of had a fling for a while. Right up until you and I got really serious actually. I ended things with him."

He sat right up. "Jocelyn, what are you saying to me? How could you get involved with that guy?"

"I'm sorry. I had just met you and you were so great but I was still tangled up with him. I didn't tell you because I didn't want to hurt you."

"So why are you telling me now?"

"I just want things to be perfect between us. I don't want to feel guilt and remorse throughout our marriage. It's out in the open now and I want us to be able to move on from this, because it really is nothing."

She could tell he was very angry with her and he had every right to be.

"I can't believe you did that Jocelyn."

"Baby, please I'm so sorry. I would never purposely hurt you."

She kissed his cheek and took his chin in her hand and forced him to look her in the eyes. "I would never hurt you. Please forgive me."

"You're going to be my wife Jocelyn of course I forgive you. You just bruised my ego a bit."

"There is no need for that. You are the only one that I want." She kissed him again and nuzzled against his chin as he shut off the TV and they went to bed. She knew it wasn't as easy as that. That he would probably lay awake all night thinking about her and Hendrick, but there was nothing she could do about it now. She would just love him as much as she could and make him forget it.

The wedding is tomorrow, holy crap, she thought. She had been rushing around all day trying to get the last minute details down. She was exhausted. She was looking forward to a peaceful night at home relaxing before she married the man of her dreams in the morning. The bridal party wanted to take her out for dinner and hang out all evening but it wasn't how she wanted to spend her last night. She would be leaving her apartment in a couple of weeks and she just wanted to enjoy it for a moment. She was going to open a bottle of wine and relish her night alone.

Tim had wanted to get married right away; he had even suggested eloping. Her father however would have murdered her so the answer was no. She could however give him a quickie wedding. After meeting with a wedding planner they had a date set for a month and a half later. Invites and announcements were sent out immediately.

The planning went flawlessly and she didn't feel at all like she had been a Bridezilla. Maybe happiness does that to a person. Her parents had accepted Tim with open arms not concerned at all with the speed in which the wedding happened, which said a lot for Tim's character.

When she finally arrived at her apartment she was tired and so looking forward to that bottle of wine. At least everything was in order as it should be. The wedding would be wonderfully perfect and they would be flying out for Paris, France immediately afterwards. The thought of Paris, the city of love, just tickled her right around insane. She couldn't wait to experience that with Tim.

She opened the door to her place, set her bags down and finally sighed with relief. Everything was finished; she just had to wait until morning to get married.

She was uncorking the bottle of wine when there was a knock on the door. Puzzled, she couldn't imagine who would be showing up now. Everyone knew she was getting married tomorrow so they would just assume she didn't want company.

She set the bottle down, and poured a tall glass before going to answer the door. When the door swung open, the glass of wine fell from her hand and smashed on the floor.

"Hendrick, what the hell do you think you are doing here!"

Leaving him at the door stunned, she stomped to the kitchen to retrieve a dustpan and some paper towels. When she returned to the door he was still in the same spot but he offered to clean up the mess for her. She was shaking all over. She was furious that he was there and even more mad at herself when she realized she loved him the moment she saw his face on the other side of the door.

He cleaned everything up and followed her into the living room.

"You better explain to me what you are doing here!"

"I love you."

"Don't you dare say those words to me."

"It's true. I'm sorry, I've been an ass. I tried to fight my feelings for so long and then I saw your wedding announcement and I lost my mind."

"How can you do this to me? It's the night before my wedding."

"I know. I'm disgusting for doing this. I thought I could let you go. But Jocelyn I can't. I need you."

"You should have thought of that months before this," she screamed the words in his face.

"You can't marry this guy."

"Why not? He's going to give me everything you weren't willing to."

"Because you are in love with me too. It's not fair to him."

She threw her hands up in the air. "Like you know anything about being fair."

They stood there staring at each other; Jocelyn's blood pressure was through the roof and he just stood there as calm as can be.

"Hendrick, how could you?" she whispered.

He shrugged. "I am sorry Jocelyn, I wish I would have told you months ago how I felt, but to be honest I thought I had a little more time to figure things out. Like, you don't think you guys might be rushing things a bit here?"

Anger boiled up in her once again. "No, I don't."

"Come on Jocelyn, he's trapping you so you can't find anyone else. That's the only reason why a guy would get married so quick."

"He's not insecure Hendrick, far from it."

"How long have you guys even known each other? Under six months to be sure."

"That doesn't matter. It doesn't change how I feel about him."

His eyes grew angry and she could tell he was holding back some biting comments. The idea of her and another man probably drove him insane.

"How do you feel about me?"

"I want you to leave. My feelings for you don't matter because I am about to marry another man tomorrow."

"I want you to change your mind. Have a future with me instead."

She stared at him and her mind was doing flip-flops while her heart ached for him. There was a part of her, and it would probably always be there, that wanted to run off into the sunset with him. But the truth of the matter was she couldn't trust him. She knew there was a chance she could give up everything for him even now and he would end up flaking out again leaving her alone.

"I tried that already Hendrick. You said you wanted to take things slow. You said you weren't ready."

"So you run off with the first available man that comes around?" he boomed.

"I love him Hendrick. You will not speak that way about him."

"Ya well you love me too, so what are you going to do about that part?"

"Nothing. It will die out eventually."

He snorted, "You and I both know that whatever there is between us will never die out. You can feel it right now can't you? The charge that is between us."

"It doesn't matter. It's too late now."

"Don't do this Jocelyn, please we could be incredible together."

"You're right. We could have been, and I feel like I really tried to have that with you Hendrick. Now I have it with Tim and I'm not going to hurt him for anything."

"You don't belong with a guy like that, you belong with me."

Her heart tore up and her mind began to fog. She didn't know what to do, what to say, or how to get him out of her apartment. God, if Tim decided to surprise her it would be all over with for sure. Maybe that's why Hendrick was there, maybe he was hoping Tim would be there.

"Please leave."

"Jocelyn..."

She looked up into his eyes. "I'm marrying Tim. Now show me some respect and please leave."

He walked away and she followed him to the door. He left silently as she closed the door behind him, locking it. She put her forehead against the door, a tear streaming down her face and whispered, "Goodbye Hendrick."

-To be continued in Book 3-

Book Three – Love Amiss

Chapter One

JOCELYN AWOKE in the arms of her husband, trying to get rid of the dream that had been plaguing her for weeks. She had now been married for six months to Tim and things weren't going quite as well as she imagined. She started having dreams about Hendrick and she figured it had to do with the fact that her unhappiness level had increased significantly.

It hadn't started out that way; they had returned from their honeymoon and she had moved into his apartment. It was bittersweet leaving her own apartment but she was excited for the future. They began immediately looking for a home to call their own. It wasn't long before they found one they both loved in the country. It was your typical colonial home in all its grandeur. There was a huge guest home in the back of the property that she couldn't wait to use. It allowed peace for themselves as well as their guests. She had a studio as well, but she still managed to drive in every day to her own studio, because she thought better and creation happened as it should.

They had lived in absolute bliss for about a month before things started to change. She wasn't really sure why the change occurred at all. Nothing negative had happened between them; one day things were just different. Tim made her insanely happy and she never regretted for a minute her decision to marry him.

He was attentive and kind and treated her like a queen. She felt safe in his arms and their sex life couldn't have been more fulfilling. He did things to her body and mind that would shock people, but it felt incredible. So, why did he have to go and ruin everything?

She didn't want to be thinking about her past flame, but Tim had changed so much in the past six months she barely recognized him. It was such a short period of time too that she didn't understand why he had proposed at all if things soured for him so quickly and easily. It made her wonder if she had made the right choice after all.

It seemed like they had the perfect marriage for about a month; they spent all their time together, going to events and parties. She often went to football games when he made appearances, which were so much fun to be around because of the noise and energy of the games. They were an amazing team. Then one day he started asking her questions about Hendrick. How long they had been together, why they ended things, how many times they had sex?

She had been shocked at first by his questions and refused to answer them. Her past shouldn't matter she had yelled at him. He was sure that she was still hung up on Hendrick despite the fact that she hadn't spoken to him since the night before their wedding. She asked him to drop it and be happy that they were together and at first he did, but his insecurities crept back in weekly, threatening to destroy them forever.

After a while his badgering continued to the point where she avoided going to events with him out of fear that they would run into Hendrick. He had been in the news a lot in the past months due to his philanthropy. She wondered if the fact that he was so visible had sparked Tim's curiosity. She had ended up telling Tim everything about her and Hendrick in the hopes that he would finally let it drop, but it only made matters worse. So she was now on a daily mission to make him happy and help him to forget there ever was another man.

She had some news to share with him when he returned from work that day that just might change everything for them. Something had to give or they would be over.

She had just started to whip up some chicken and dumplings with a salad for dinner when he came through the door.

His face lit up when he saw her and she hoped that it was going to be a good night for them.

"Jose, you look beautiful as always. How was your day?"

He walked over to her, kissing her on the lips. She smiled, "I had a great day. Work went great and I got out of the studio early to make my handsome husband a home-cooked meal for once."

He laughed, "Well I appreciate it, my love."

He presented her with a red velvet box. "What's this?" she asked.

"It's an apology. I've been an idiot for a while and I don't want to lose you."

"I married you Tim, you aren't going to lose me."

"I've been crazy about your involvement with Hendrick, worried that it was him you really wanted and that you would leave me for him, and I've driven you nuts about it too."

A tear rolled down Jocelyn's cheek and he quickly wiped it away. "Please don't cry. I'm sorry. I've pushed you away, I just hope we can repair the damage I caused."

She opened up the box to find a diamond bracelet. She kissed him on the mouth and he hugged her tight.

"I may have some news that would be a great start to a new future."

He raised an eyebrow, still holding her close he asked, "Oh really and what's that?"

She looked deep into his eyes as she whispered, "I'm pregnant."

He looked so shocked it was almost comical.

She laughed, and he laughed along with her. "I'm sorry darling, I didn't expect that at all."

"But you're happy right?"

He grinned, "Are you kidding me, that's the best news I've ever heard. I'm a very lucky guy."

"Everything is going to be perfect Tim, I love you."

"I love you too."

He kissed her again and lingered with it, slowly slipping his tongue into her mouth. She accepted it and sucked gently on it. His arms wrapped around her and his hands found their way to her ass. She kissed him more intensely and began rubbing his cock through his pants. It wasn't long before he was hard as a rock, a very big rock. He moaned with the friction her hand was causing.

"I'm going to fuck you so good, baby."

She moaned, excitement igniting her. He lifted her into his arms and carried her to their bedroom. He laid her down on the bed and watched as she undressed before him. He began to take off his shirt, then his pants and watched as she spread her legs revealing her opening. She was giving him motivation to hurry. He bent down before her and lapped away at her pussy. She tasted so sweet and soft beneath his tongue.

Jocelyn moaned. Things in the bedroom had become pretty aggressive, not that she minded but it was certainly a change. She knew it probably had to do with his need to claim her in his own mind and she allowed it in the hopes that it made him feel confident.

He sucked on her clit, slowly putting two fingers inside her. She gasped and he pumped into her hard, her mind swirling with the intensity building up inside her. She knew what was coming: he would slide his cock hard into her and claim her once again. Tim was very well endowed and it was always an overwhelming feeling to have him enter her. In a good way no doubt, he hit every nerve inside her when they fucked.

He raised himself up. "Turn over baby I want to fuck you doggy."

She immediately turned over and pushed her bum in the air. "Fuck me Tim, really good."

That was all the encouragement he needed to plunge his throbbing cock inside her.

She cried out with the pressure of his size pushing into her. He pushed into her deeper and she moaned loudly. Having him inside her drove her mad, she felt wanton with such a cock pumping hard inside her. She couldn't get enough of him.

"Please Tim, I need it."

He pounded roughly against her and she moaned with every thrust. He rubbed her ass, his most favorite attribute of hers. He slowed his thrusts moving in and out of her slowly but going deeper inside with everyone.

"Tim, god baby you feel so good."

"Your pussy feels incredible Jose."

He leaned over to their nightstand and picked up a butt plug. He slowly inserted it into her bum. She moaned feeling filled in both areas. They had started having anal sex upon his request a few months ago and due to his size they always started off with a butt plug to open her up a bit.

He fucked her slowly with both his cock and the plug. She thought she was going to lose her mind there were so many delicious sensations.

He slowly pulled the plug out and then his cock from her pussy. She knew what was coming and she tried to remain relaxed to make the transition easier. He slowly entered her ass and she cried out with pleasure. The combination of pain and pleasure thrilled her. He bent over further and bit her on the shoulder. She was delirious with pleasure and she thought she would lose her mind when the full length of him started pumping into her slowly.

"There you go baby, that feels good doesn't it?"

"Oh Tim, your cock makes me feel so good."

He found her clit underneath and rubbed into her as his pace picked up. She felt a tension building inside her and he often made her cum with his cock in her ass. It felt so good.

"Oh Tim, I'm going to cum."

He pumped into her until she came and then he spilled himself into her bum. He pulled out of her and they jumped into the shower together.

She soaped him up and his hands went to her stomach. "It's real isn't it?"

She smiled, "Yes my love, everything is going to be different."

Jocelyn's pregnancy flew by. She had the most incredible baby shower that her husband and best friend arranged. There were over 200 people there and she had to admit it was a little overwhelming. The child they had would have enough clothes until college.

What a whirlwind though, so much to do in so little time. Her clothing line was getting picked up more and more by celebrities and she was starting to become part of the elite designers. As soon as she found out she was pregnant she started a couture line for little girls and boys. She was going to launch it once the baby arrived. She already had standing orders from celebrities who felt they shouldn't have to wait for the launch. She wasn't ready yet and those orders would not be going through until the baby was born. Everything had to be just right before she would launch and right now she needed to focus on Tim. He had been very different since she told him she was pregnant, it seemed to have done the trick to bring him back to her.

She was due in a couple of days and she was anxious to get that part over with. Please, bring on the baby part, this pregnancy stuff is for the birds. She was achy and tired and wanted a glass of wine. She and Tim had been having sex a few times a day in the hopes of inducing her but nothing had worked so far. She was surprised since sex with Tim was always a little rough.

When she woke up the next morning, she lumbered her way out of bed and feeling like a beached whale, she made her way to the bathroom. She was brushing her teeth when she felt a pop and then something trickled down her leg. She stopped and wondered about the weird sensation. She bent down to look and saw a puddle on the floor. She expected it to be more dramatic, like a flood but sure enough her water had broken.

She hurried out of the bathroom and grabbed her phone to call Tim. He picked up immediately and told her he would have his driver bring her to the hospital and he would meet her there. She grabbed her overnight bag and headed to the lobby.

Chapter Two

Her labor had been five hours long and considering it was a drug free labor it had been the longest five hours of her life. She had a private suite that was all so luxurious. The room she was in was the size of her master bedroom at home. She had everything in there that she could possibly ever need to be comfortable. She had a full staff of nurses as well as her doctor checked in on her regularly. Tim swept into the room holding a little bundle.

"I managed to snag her away. They are done with her checkup so she can stay in here with us now."

"Bring her to me." She nuzzled the little girl, kissing her little face.

"She's so beautiful Tim."

"Of course she is, look at her mother."

She smiled as he kissed her on the forehead.

"Have you chosen a name for our perfect little girl yet?"

"Yes actually I have. Jasmine."

His face lit up, "That's beautiful and just perfect."

Just then one of the nurses came in carrying a rather large package, with a "It's A Girl" balloon.

She sat it down on a side table in the room. "Lucky girl, I wonder who sent this," she exclaimed as she walked out the door.

Tim walked over to the basket searching for a card. It was clear that a lot of money had been spent on the basket and she couldn't imagine who would send something like that after she had already had a shower.

"There's a note, but no name with it. Who would send an anonymous present?" he asked her.

"I have no idea! Aside from maybe flowers I didn't expect anything to come in today." She watched as he looked in the basket and thought it weird that he hadn't brought it over to her yet.

"Very, very expensive stuff."

"Can I see it Tim?"

He didn't answer her and instead continued to look through the basket.

He spun around with an angry look on his face. "It's from him isn't it?"

She stared at him not understanding, "Who?"

"You know who I'm talking about."

"No actually Tim, I have no idea why you are flying off the handle right now. I would like to see the package, what is wrong with you?"

He laughed, "Ya I bet you do."

She stared, her mouth hanging open. Tears began forming in her eyes. "Tim, what's wrong?"

"Hendrick sent this, didn't he?"

She laughed even though it wasn't laughable at all. "Are you joking? I have no idea who sent it. I haven't talked to Hendrick since before we were married."

"If it wasn't for our daughter's skin color I would have to start wondering if she was even mine."

Shock rendered Jocelyn speechless and tears streamed down her face. She had a hard time forming words. "How could you say something like that to me?"

His hands flung up in the air and he stormed from the room.

"Tim!!" she called after him.

He didn't come back. She sat there rocking Jasmine trying to figure out what had just happened to her life. She got up and set Jasmine in the bassinet to sleep so she could check out the package. It was elaborate to be sure and she had to wonder herself if Hendrick was behind it. She didn't know anyone who would send diamond studs for a newborn. Someone with a lot of money to burn, that's for sure.

"I hope you like the package."

Startled she spun around to find Hendrick in her room. Her heart slammed against her chest and she relived the last night she saw him all over again. After all this time she still had feelings for him.

"Oh god Hendrick what are you doing here? Are you trying to get me divorced?" Tears streamed down her face.

He was by her side in a second. He pulled her into his arms. "Jocelyn what's wrong? I'm so sorry. I didn't mean to upset you so. This is supposed to be a happy day."

"He saw your package, he lost his mind. He left the hospital. I don't know what he will do if he sees you in here with me."

Anger crossed Hendrick's face. "Who the hell is this guy? He doesn't sound like he's very nice to you."

Jocelyn cried harder. "Look I'm sorry I sent the package without a name, I thought that would be enough. But still I didn't expect such an extreme reaction. I didn't send the package to be an ass, Jocelyn. I sent it because I care about you and wanted to congratulate you."

She looked up into his eyes. "What if he finds you here?"

"He won't, I have someone watching the building. That's how I knew it was safe to come up."

She groaned, "Hendrick, you were just waiting outside until you could come in? You're impossible."

"Not impossible, just determined to see you and your new bundle."

"Speaking of my bundle, how did you know I had a girl? I barely just found out myself," she laughed.

"I told you, I like to know things. I've kept a tab on you for a while Jocelyn, I wanted to make sure you were happy and taken care of."

"We've had our problems."

"You sure haven't been together long for that. And leaving you at the hospital Jocelyn is a huge dick move on his part."

"He's obsessed with you. You drive him insane."

"Maybe he knows he doesn't deserve you."

"Hendrick please, let's not make this difficult. Tim is a good man. He's just allowed his jealousy to control our relationship. We weren't even together long, I don't know why you bother him so much."

She watched as he walked to the bassinet and peeked inside. His face opened up into a huge smile. "She is beautiful Jocelyn, she looks just like you." She was surprised to see him reach in and pick Jasmine up. She knew how Hendrick felt about her and she expected him to be put off by another man's baby but he didn't seem fazed at all by it.

"Thank you, her name is Jasmine."

"She's so tiny," he laughed holding Jasmine in his arms.

Tears streamed down her face as she looked at them beautiful together.

"I made the wrong choice didn't I? I loved him so much but I made the wrong choice."

Shocked, Hendrick didn't say a word. He set Jasmine back down to sleep and came over to Jocelyn.

"Believe me if there's any fault here it's all mine. I should have told you how I really felt before it was too late. I waited too long and I don't blame you for choosing someone else."

He pulled her in for a hug and let her sob into his chest.

"I'm so sorry, Jocelyn. My intention was not to hurt you today. I just wanted to see you."

His phone beeped and he knew that meant that Tim was on his way back into the hospital.

She pulled away from him and he whispered, "Please, you have a beautiful baby, enjoy her. I'm sorry."

They kissed on the lips, and she suddenly felt whole again.

Then he left quickly as if he was never there at all. She sat on the bed and wiped her tears, trying to compose herself.

It wasn't 15 minutes later that Tim came back into the room with flowers in hand. So that explained Hendrick's hasty retreat. She couldn't even imagine what Tim would have done had he found Hendrick there; murder was certainly a huge possibility.

"I am so sorry." Tim came over to her and she put her hands up to keep him back.

"Oh no you don't. You don't get to say those things to me and then bring flowers like you didn't just behave like a dick on the birthday of our daughter."

He stood there unsure of how to proceed. She had never talked that way to him before, but she was sick of being treated like a doormat because of his jealousy.

"You will earn your place by my side or get out of my life. You will get a handle on your jealousy or leave."

She walked past him and got back into bed. She wanted to rest before Jasmine awoke again.

Chapter Three

Six months passed and Jocelyn was at home getting ready for an AIDS benefit. She had finally lost all her baby weight and intended on looking fine in the full-length black lace gown Tim had bought her for the occasion. They hadn't been out together in ages, as Tim had been working so much lately that he came home late most nights. After their little spat at the hospital, things got back on track with them and she really believed everything was going to be great. It wasn't until one night when they went out and got a little tipsy that he had then started in about Hendrick again. She just felt like giving up. After that, she saw less and less of him. For the past three months he had been working late at least four days a week. She had to sometimes bring Jasmine into his office just so the poor thing could spend some time with her daddy. He didn't seem to get that Jasmine needed to see her dad sometimes too, or that she was more important than his career. It certainly wasn't about the money. They had more than she could ever ask for.

Tim came in then smiling at her. He came over and kissed the side of her mouth.

"You look incredible Jocelyn."

"Thank you sweetheart, I feel incredible."

They laughed together and he hugged her tight. "I'm looking forward to being out with you tonight. It's been awhile for us."

She nodded sadly.

"I'm trying to make a good life for us."

"No Tim, we already have a good life. You are off doing something else. It's time you come back to us and leave someone else to do the work. You're the boss, right?"

"I know. You're right."

The benefit was being held at one of the swankiest hotels in town and the dining area was to die for. Jocelyn smiled as soon as she entered. Well this was certainly the life. Tickets for this event were a thousand dollars apiece, but it was all for charity so Jocelyn didn't mind. She was surprised to see little miss rock star there as well and as pregnant as can be.

"Jocelyn! You look amazing. You must tell me how you got your baby weight off."

Jocelyn giggled, "It was no easy task let me tell you."

"When this little bugger pops out I want in on your junior line, it's so chic!"

"Of course. Do you know what you're having?"

"A girl, of course, I can't wait to take her shopping," she squealed.

Jocelyn excused herself from the conversation and made a mental note to send the rock star a baby shower basket to keep her focused on her line and only hers.

Tim and Jocelyn were about to reach their table when Hendrick approached them. Jocelyn had wondered if he would be there and sure enough there he was. It just amazed her that he had the balls to approach them.

"Hello Tim and Jocelyn, I'm glad to see you both here. It probably brings you back to the olden days?"

Jocelyn laughed, "Yes, I would actually like to go back sometime but Jasmine is just too young right now."

"You should have brought her, I would have loved to have met her."

"No, babies and benefits don't go well together."

"Fair enough."

The whole time Tim didn't smile or speak a word. It annoyed Jocelyn immensely.

Hendrick met Tim's eyes and said, "Hey, your team has done fantastic this year, congrats."

Jocelyn was surprised to see Tim glaring at Hendrick.

"I want you to stay away from my family, do you hear me?" Tim seethed the words out in a hiss.

Hendrick was taken aback and that was all it took for Jocelyn to say something.

"Tim, you're out of line. You're being very rude."

"No, what amazes me, Jocelyn, is how you stick up for this pig every chance you get."

Appalled, Jocelyn took a step back and she could tell Hendrick was holding back some biting words.

"If you two will excuse me, this pig is going to get a drink."

Jocelyn almost laughed except she was furious with Tim. She turned to him. "What is the matter with you?"

"Don't start Jocelyn, don't you start."

"Do you realize it has been almost two years since I was involved with Hendrick? And even then, it was brief. Two years and you are still making a fool of yourself over him."

She turned and walked away from him, needing her distance.

Heading to the bar in desperate need of a stiff drink, she walked right into Hendrick.

"My god, are you just everywhere?" she said annoyed.

"Ouch. No need to be mean, Jocelyn."

"Well why the hell did you have to come and say hello anyways?"

He laughed, "Oh well I'm sorry. Maybe I'm just too much of a nice guy."

"Please, let's not get carried away with that. You're not that nice."

"Well maybe you're right."

"Tim walked away from me."

She sidled up to the bar and ordered a drink. As she waited with Hendrick he whispered. "He's gone Jocelyn."

She turned to him with a look that should have instilled fear. "What did you say to me?"

"He left, Jocelyn. Right after the argument, he walked right out to his car and he hasn't come back in."

"You're lying."

"No, he left you here alone. Again."

She pulled out her phone and dialed her husband. It went straight to voicemail. Her heart plummeted. He never shut his phone off, especially if he was out with her. Sometimes they got separated and needed to find each other, and calling was the best way to do it. She tried his phone again and came up with the same result. Her drink had arrived and she downed it in one gulp. She ordered another and attempted to sip at it.

"You look absolutely stunning by the way. If that makes you feel any better," he joked, trying to make her smile. She couldn't however. All she wanted to do was choke her own husband. What was the matter with him? How could he keep doing this to her?

"Well it certainly can't hurt." She finished her drink and ordered another.

"Maybe you should take it easy Jocelyn."

"Don't tell me what to do."

"You getting drunk is not going to help."

"I think you need to take me somewhere else."

He looked her in the eyes, held her gaze, not wavering. "Are you sure?"

"Yes, I need to get out of here."

He took her hand and led her out of the dining room. "Wait here." She stood outside the door while Hendrick disappeared. It wasn't long before Hendrick returned. "Let's go."

She followed him, unsure of why she was following him and unsure of where they were going. They walked to the elevator together and rode up to the penthouse suite of that luxurious hotel. She wasn't sure what was going to happen once they got up to his suite, but she didn't care at that point. She was furious at Tim, and she couldn't imagine that they could continue on the way they were going.

She walked around the suite and he came up behind her, putting his mouth on her shoulder. She turned around to face him and kissed him full on the mouth. Their tongues melded together with heat building up between them. She moaned, aching in every part of her body for him. He kissed her mouth, her chin and lingered on her neck nipping his way down. She was throbbing all over for him.

"Please, I need you now. Please don't make me wait."

He picked her up and carried her to the master bedroom. She noticed the room had items scattered in it.

"Have you been staying here?"

"No, but I did plan on having you here. And I want to claim you as mine."

"Really? You planned to have me here?"

"Well I didn't think Tim would make it quite so easy, but yes I did have the intention of making you mine again, in body if not in mind."

"I missed you Hendrick."

"God darling I missed you too."

"It looks like you have something rough in store for me."

"Well I think you've been bad, darling, keeping me away from your beautiful pussy for so long. I haven't stopped thinking about you in two years."

"Bad?"

"Yes and you need to be punished. A good... hard punishing should make you see where you belong."

She couldn't believe how wet she was getting just from him talking to her. She began to undress, sliding the straps of her lace gown off her shoulders and letting the gown fall to the floor. She was completely nude underneath the dress and she smiled as he looked her over. He undressed showing her a completely rock hard cock ready to punish her just the way he wanted.

He led her to the bed and bent her over. She knew he was going to take her from behind. He picked up a paddle and slapped her bottom with it. She gasped and swore she could cum just like that.

"You're mine, Jocelyn."

She moaned.

"Say it. Tell me your mine."

"I'm yours, Hendrick. I'm all yours. Take me."

He paddled her ass again and drove his cock into her. She cried out and he plunged in deeper and deeper every time. She was moaning so loudly that he thought he would lose his mind. It was the best sound in the world.

He pushed in a butt plug while he fucked her. She was getting hit in various nerves while he fucked her quite perfectly. She didn't know how much she could take and she came all over his cock. He flipped her over, putting his hands around her throat; her voice caught just as he plunged his cock into her. She got completely foggy and lightheaded, and thought she would pass out. He released her throat, pumping inside her hard and fast. She came so hard her whole body rocked. Hendrick fucked her with the butt plug while tantalizing her pussy with his hard cock.

"Oh Hendrick, you feel so good, I can't stand it."

"Oh baby, you are perfect. Every part of you. You are so wet I need to be inside you all the time."

She came again, feeling completely taken by this man; she didn't know if she could ever leave his side again. He had stayed with her for years, just waiting for her.

He filled her full of cum and collapsed on top of her. She kissed the top of his head trying to catch her breath.

They lay there for an hour, not speaking, just holding each other tight. She wasn't sure what was going to happen next. She didn't know what was right and what was wrong anymore. All her decisions had still led to this moment there with Hendrick. This moment where she knew she could never go back. It had always been Hendrick, he had stood by her no matter what her decisions were, while her husband sabotaged every moment they had together with jealousy. She had thought having the baby would have completed their family and killed all the jealousy, but it hadn't. He had allowed his jealousy to poison their relationship to the point where he was hardly at home to even see his daughter. She knew she couldn't live like that anymore. Jocelyn knew she had put her fair effort into the relationship and shouldn't feel any guilt in leaving. But she did, because she loved him and she knew deep down he loved her and that his worst fears would come true when she walked out on him. It would be even worse to find out that she eventually ended up with Hendrick anyways; it would surely kill him. But she had made the wrong choice once already, she wasn't about to do it again. She was going to start living the life she wanted, the life she should have had from the beginning. She was done choosing the wrong man; she would grab a hold of Hendrick and never let him go. It was her turn to shine and be loved in the way she deserved.

"I need to go Hendrick."

"Where?"

"You know where."

"Let me get dressed and I will come with you."

She laughed, "You know that's not going to happen."

"I would stand beside you up against any adversary."

She looked into his eyes and smiled. "I know you would, but this is something I need to do on my own, for me."

"I'm here if you need me, I won't leave this room until I hear from you."

She kissed him on the mouth, jumping out of bed to get dressed. She wasn't looking forward to finding Tim, but it had to be done. She said goodbye and headed for the door.

Chapter Four

When she returned home she was surprised to find Tim was not there. Where had he gone after the benefit? He must have gone to the office and buried himself in work to forget they had any problems. She quickly messaged Hendrick and told him she was going to bed, that she had not found Tim. She paid the sitter then went to go check on Jasmine.

Her cute little bundle slept soundly in her crib. She grew more beautiful by the day and Jocelyn counted her blessings everyday that Jasmine was brought into her life. The one thing she didn't regret from the whole marriage was her precious daughter. She was proof that love truly does prevail through misery and destruction. She kissed her daughter on the forehead, careful not to wake her. She went to her bedroom, undressed and fell exhausted into bed. She fell asleep as soon as her head hit the pillow.

It was early when Tim awoke Jocelyn from her sleep. Bleary-eyed, she rolled over groaning.

"I made you some coffee, get up love."

She sat up in the bed, propping herself up against the pillows. She was still exhausted and in no mood to be woken up so early.

"Where is Jasmine?"

"Your parents came to pick her up for the day."

"It's kind of early, why would they do that?"

"Well I asked them to."

She stared at him and knew this was not going to be a conversation she liked. It was too early and the caffeine was not in her veins yet. "I'm not in the mood for whatever you have planned for me Tim, I'm exhausted."

"You don't think we should talk about last night?"

She looked over at the clock, her blood starting to boil. "At 6am? That's when you think we need to have a talk about last night. None of my brain cells are working right now Tim."

"I'm sorry, I can't wait, I have been up all night."

"Yes well speaking of that, where were you last night because I know you didn't come back home. Why would you walk out of the benefit like that, and just leave me there without telling me?"

"I just can't take him talking to you. And you should respect that."

"Oh Tim, grow up. I didn't approach him, he came to me and I'm not going to be rude to a man that has done nothing wrong to either of us. He didn't steal me away Tim, I've always been with you."

"Well except for last night."

"What does that mean?"

"It means, I returned to the benefit to apologize and you were gone."

She was stunned. "Oh wow big surprise. I'm sure you think it must mean something that you come back after ditching me to apologize for being a huge dick."

"I overreacted."

"That's an understatement."

"Where were you? Why did you leave the hotel?"

She paused, unable to believe she was going to say it. "I didn't leave the hotel. I just wasn't where you wanted me to be."

They stared at each other in silence, neither of them willing to break it for fear there would be an explosion.

"Why, Jocelyn?"

"I got tired of waiting for my husband to start acting like a husband."

"Excuse me?"

"What happened to you? What happened to that charming, confident, amazing man that I met? That was the one I thought I was marrying, but instead I got a controlling, weak, insecure man. A man who worried so much about another man that he destroyed a perfectly good, loving marriage."

"You always wanted him."

"No Tim. I wanted you, I married you."

"Then why are you leaving me for him now?"

"Cause I deserve the best and I thought that was you, but it turns out I was wrong."

"Please Jocelyn, don't go. I can change. I don't want to lose you."

"I'm sorry, Tim. You should have changed years ago. It's too late."

"Have you always loved him?"

"I've always had feelings for him, yes. But let me make something clear to you. It doesn't minimize what we had. When I married you I wanted you and the life I thought we could have together. I loved you Tim, but that's not enough to keep me living like this."

He put his head in his hands as she got up to shower; she had to start making some plans and it started with Tim leaving.

"I'm sorry Tim, but you will need to stay in the guest house until we have things figured out. I need to be here with Jasmine and I'm not moving out until I've found a suitable place for us to live."

He just nodded and she headed to the shower.

<<<>>>

Starting a new life had its challenges, and her parents begged her to stay married and work it out with Tim. They were old fashioned, plus they really liked him. She couldn't blame them; on the outside everything had looked perfect. But perfect it was not. To make matters worse she eventually moved into a home that Hendrick purchased for them. They had not known anything about Hendrick and here she was moving in with him while her divorce went through.

Jasmine came with her of course, and Hendrick adored her just as much as he did her mother. She hadn't been sure what Hendrick would be like as a father, but it turned out she had nothing to worry about, he was a natural. He had no issue with helping her raise her daughter though Jasmine didn't need a dad, as Tim was still very much in the picture.

Jocelyn couldn't have dreamed that things would turn out the way they did, but she was blissfully happy with an amazing man by her side finally. She wouldn't change anything about the life that got her to this moment.

-The End-

If you enjoyed this series, I would appreciate your leaving a review of the book. Good reviews encourage an author to write as well as help books to sell. Good reviews can be just a few short sentences describing what you liked about the book without having a spoiler. If you could spend 30 seconds writing a review, I would appreciate it: you can review this title right now at your favorite retailer.

Here is a preview of **another story** you may enjoy:

Love Anew - Lonely Billionaire Romance Series, Book 1

TRICIA REACHED for another blanket. "Are you cold?" she asked.

Rebecca's breath was raspy as she responded. As her lungs shut down due to ALS, or Amyotrophic Lateral Sclerosis, her ability to speak had started to decline. Muscle by muscle, ALS targeted the body and made it impossible for the individual to live a normal life. It had started a few years ago with Rebecca's legs. Now, her lung muscles were starting to freeze as well. Tricia winced as she thought about the future. If Rebecca chose to use machines to stay alive, her entire body would eventually stop working. At some point, her mind would remain functioning and she would be locked into her body.

Rebecca managed to squeeze out a feeble yes. Reaching over to the cupboard, Tricia removed a blanket and carefully tucked her in. Tricia had spent years training to be a nurse and really liked her job. Since she was an excellent nurse, she had caught the eye of the billionaire, John, at one of the couple's many trips to hospitals around the country. He had noticed the love and care she took with each patient. After a moment's hesitation, Tricia had allowed him to convince her to take care of his wife.

Pictures of Rebecca dotted the room. Since she was unable to leave, John had striven to make her room look like favorite memories of her life and activities. A young, healthy Rebecca smiled in each photo. In the few years she had been physically active, she had acquired awards for horseback riding, cooking and other projects. Now, though, this time of physical fitness had passed. Instead of dashing through the fields on her favorite horse, Rebecca spent her time in this room. She had taken her difficulties in stride and was truly brave in the face of all of these medical issues.

Finishing with the blanket, Rebecca started to say something. Leaning closer to hear her, Tricia finally pulled up a chair. "What do you need, Rebecca?" she queried.

Sighing, Rebecca whispered, "I need to talk to John. I have to tell him how I want to die."

Squeezing her hand, Tricia nodded. "Once I leave your room, I will go get him. Just in case he is not around, did you want me to give him a message?"

Rebecca tried to nod, but her head did not respond all the way. "Yes, I do. You need to tell him that I do not want any machines. He could keep me alive forever with a breathing tube, but I do not want to live a life where I am permanently locked into my body. And," she paused and struggled to take another breath. "I do not want him to stop enjoying life or waiting around for my eventual death. If God wants to take my soul now, we should not interfere."

Tricia nodded sadly. Most patients with ALS were more afraid of being stuck within their minds than actual death. She understood, but she could not imagine what life would be like without Rebecca's gentle soul. "I will tell him," she said.

Leaving the room, Tricia traversed the hallways of the mansion. John had built his fortune by buying and selling real estate properties. His initial money had arrived through an early investment in the dot com boom before the bubble burst. After seeing the dangers of the stock market, he had started to just buy and rent out properties. Even with the recent recession, he still made a profit. Instead of selling his properties or developing, he had continued to rent them out. In a decade or two, he had talked of selling and retiring. His plans had arrived before his wife had been diagnosed with ALS. Unwilling to speak of his life after her future death, Tricia had not asked about any change in his future plans.

The halls of the house were dotted with white oak doorways that led to a myriad of rooms. Plush white carpet softly surrounded Tricia's feet as she walked. She dreaded the conversation that was about to happen. Every day, she updated John about the status of his wife. Unfortunately, she seldom had good news to share. She nodded to John's secretary as she entered the office. Unlike most rich men, he used a male secretary. Before talking had become so difficult, Rebecca had explained that he tried to hire primarily males so that Rebecca would never worry about his fidelity. Since Tricia was intended to cater just to his wife, she had been allowed to work there despite her gender.

If you enjoyed this sample then look for **Love Anew - Lonely Billionaire Romance Series, Book 1.**

Here is a preview of **another book** you may also enjoy:

Love Eluded - Audacious Billionaire BWWM Romance Series, Book 1

CHANTE GREEN knew she was going to be late for work…again.

"Shit…," she mumbled, impatiently tapping her foot as she craned her neck to see if the bus was anywhere in sight.

She could almost see the look of annoyance on the face of her supervisor, Nurse Betty Lebowitz. It was the third time this month alone and Chante knew she was hanging by a thread. She could lose her job at New York General Hospital, and she needed that now more than ever.

Chante genuinely hoped that Nurse Betty would be a little sympathetic and cut her some slack. After all, the supervisor was familiar with the reason Chante was under a tremendous amount of pressure. Her brother Markey had ALS or Amyotrophic Lateral Sclerosis, also known as Lou Gehrig's disease.

A catastrophic disease that was initially misdiagnosed, Markey now had only partial control of his legs. Looking back, he was always clumsy as a child, often falling or stumbling, but everyone said it was just a phase and he'll eventually outgrow it. But as the years progressed, Chante noticed the slurred speech. Her mom eventually took him to a specialist who, after rigorous testing declared the boy was in the second stages of ALS.

Things became even more difficult when Chante's dad contracted malaria and eventually died from it.

Chante and her mom, both heartbroken over the sudden death, struggled to meet the special needs that were required to deal with ALS. Her mom, having had experience in caring for sick children, took on most of the responsibilities. When swallowing became too hard, they took turns giving him food through a feeding tube. Mom would bathe him; help him use the bathroom; exercise his arms and legs to prevent atrophy, until her son's disease took its toll on her as well.

Driving one night to buy medicine at a nearby pharmacy, she was too preoccupied to notice the red light at a street intersection and was hit on the driver's side by a passing truck. She was in a coma for three days before she succumbed to her injuries. At nineteen years old, Chante was left with an enormous responsibility towards a brother who was not even of her own blood, but who meant more to her than anything in the whole world. He was her only family.

Chante didn't remember much of her early childhood years, except shuttling from one foster home to another. At six years old, she was considered too old by most couples wanting to adopt a baby. The shy and gawky black girl with soulful green eyes was never chosen. Unable to find a good family for her, city officials decided to turn her over to the State Institution for Unwanted Children. On the eve of her departure, a woman came in, noticed her cringing in a corner, and approached her.

Chante believed she was an angel with blond hair falling softly around her shoulder. But it was the sweet voice that calmed her enough to reach for the hand that was offered to her. The woman was enamored with the emaciated child and decided to adopt her. The lady,

Hannah Green, brought her home and introduced her to her husband, Caleb, a Mulatto who was delighted to see her. Chante felt an instant kinship with the dark-skinned stranger. Hannah made her feel like the daughter they never had. Both were missionaries who went to far-flung places on medical missions.

Chante spent her growing years travelling to places most children would have found depressing. No electricity, no running water, and sometimes just a hut to sleep on at night, if they were lucky. Otherwise, it had to be in a tent or under the stars. Children with malaria, TB, pneumonia, measles, and countless other maladies constantly filled their days.

From her adoptive parents, Chante learned compassion, dedication, and sympathy for the sick. No one was turned away. There was always room for one more.

Chante blossomed under their care. The lost look in her eyes gradually changed to confidence. She learned her ABC's under Acacia trees with other children. Instead of children's books, medical books were her constant companion. She couldn't read most of the words, but the pictures amazed her. It was no surprise that she declared she would become a doctor someday. She changed her mind after she found her passion working alongside the nurses, who took care of their patients day in and day-out.

It was during one of these missions that her mom and dad discovered that they were expecting a baby. Chante's innate insecurity returned. She knew she was adopted and was afraid to be given away again. Her parents, seeing the troubled look on her face, assured her that she would always be a part of their family. They loved her so much like she was their very own, they said. That restored her confidence so much so that when the baby finally arrived, Chante immediately fell in love with the little bundle of crinkly skin and puffy eyes. No one seeing them for the first time would ever doubt they were brother and sister. They looked so much alike… same curly hair and bronzed chocolaty skin complexion.

When Chante's dad contracted malaria and eventually died from it, they moved to a smaller house. Maintaining the big sprawling colonial house where Chante grew up became too much for her mom. Money was scarce with the little pension she was receiving from her work as a missionary and Chante was in her last year in high school.

If you enjoyed this sample then look for **Love Eluded - Audacious Billionaire BWWM Romance Series, Book 1**.

Here is a preview of **another book** you may also enjoy:

Love Invested – Persuasive Billionaire BWWM Romance Series, Book 1

"**THEY'RE ASKING** for the eggs to be cooked again."

"What? Those are fine!"

"What do you want me to do about it, Brad? The customer is complaining. Just make them again, alright? He wants the eggs overcooked, apparently."

Brad took the plate from Stacey's hand and returned to his grill, grumbling loudly. Stacey wiped the sweat from her brow and turned around, getting ready to head back out onto the floor of *Papa's Grill and Diner*.

It was the middle of the day in mid-summer, which made the sweltering kitchen unbearable. Stacey was glad to leave the kitchen even if it meant dealing with a couple of jerk customers.

Back in the dining area, she looked around. She had only one couple in her section. They were older, with their shoulders hunched over and beady eyes pointed toward the kitchen. The woman hadn't touched her sandwich, probably waiting for the man to get his eggs back before digging in.

There was only one other waitress, Maria, working, and she was in the corner, texting on her phone. Their place wasn't exactly the hot spot of the city to eat during the best of times. During mid-day, it was more like a graveyard.

The woman motioned for Stacey to come over. She clenched her jaw, exhaled slowly and got ready for whatever ridiculous request the woman was going to make. This couple had been a hassle from the moment they were seated.

"How can I help you?" she asked, plastering a smile on her face.

The woman scowled, "Where are my husband's eggs?"

"They're making him a fresh batch right now."

"Tell them to hurry up!" the woman snapped.

The husband sat there silently, playing with the edge of his napkin. But he nodded at Stacey as if to tell her he better get his eggs soon.

Stacey scurried back into the kitchen. It was mind-numbing if she let it get to her. How long had she been working here now? Four years? It was supposed to be a pit stop before she moved onto bigger and better things. She had been there, scraping by, instead of returning to college or working on making something more of herself.

No use in thinking about that now.

Brad handed her a plate of freshly cooked eggs. She walked back to the table and placed it in front of the man and his wife.

The man wrinkled his nose and said, "This will do, I suppose."

Stacey clasped her hands together and inquired as politely as she could muster, "Would you like more coffee?"

They grunted, and she gave them a fresh pot, making sure not to add it their bill. She was sure they would want something for free out of the egg fiasco. By the time the couple left, Stacey was ready for a break.

In the break room, she slipped off her shoes and rubbed her feet, wincing. Her shoes were cheap, and it showed after standing in them for more than a couple of hours. Her feet were killing her.

She checked her phone next. There was a voicemail from her sister. It was a rare event that her sister reached out to her and she was filled with dread listening to the message.

"Stacey, hey. It's your sister, Allison," she added for clarification as if Stacey wouldn't know her own sister's name. "Listen, call me when you can? I have a question to ask you. Well, more of a favor? But I need to talk to you first. Thanks, bye."

Stacey sighed as the message ended. Her sister wanting a favor never led to anything good. *If she wants money, she can forget it*. There was no cash to give Allison. There were barely any funds for Stacey.

A small TV in the break room played the news. The image was grainy but she could just make out the weatherman talking about rain later on in the evening. *Great*. She made a mental note to make sure the roof didn't leak all over everything when she got home from work. Last time it stormed, Stacey had to set out buckets to catch the drips.

She closed her eyes just for a moment. If she left them closed for too long, she would fall asleep on the spot. It felt as if there was always something to do. She finished one thing, and another task popped up in its place. Maybe that was how it would always be.

"Wake up, sleepyhead."

Stacey opened her eyes to see Amanda stepping into the break room.

"You work today?" Stacey asked, surprised, wondering why they needed another waitress working during such a slow day.

"Nah, I left my wallet here last night in my locker. I was so tired after closing, it just slipped my mind." Amanda walked over to her locker and glanced back at Stacey. "You okay?"

"Yeah, just tired."

"Looks dead here. I'd be tired too," Amanda remarked as she opened up her locker.

"Yeah, it's pretty boring."

Amanda paused in front of her open locker, grabbed her wallet, and tucked it into her purse. When she turned back around, she had a strange look on her face. Stacey sat up straighter.

"What?"

Amanda hesitated and then sat down on the wooden bench. Stacey could see the purple circles under Amanda's eyes. Although they both worked full time at the restaurant, Amanda also attended college. She was probably just as tired as Stacey.

"I heard something. Probably just a rumor. I don't know. I wasn't going to tell anyone but—"

But I know how much you need this job was the unfinished thought there.

"What is it?"

Amanda lowered her voice, "Heard at a class yesterday this place might close down."

"Who was talking about that in your class?" Stacey scoffed. "Especially about our little place."

"Well, I mentioned that I work here. I was in my accounting class, and we were doing a project. This kid in my group said that I should look for other work because this place is going to shut down. Especially with all those investment groups coming in here trying to revive the area."

Stacey scowled. Her neighborhood, which was predominantly black, had indeed been crawling with rich white men in suits lately. All of them wanted to knock down and rebuild her section of town. They wanted to make it new and fresh again. They wanted it to appeal to the elite, which naturally meant getting rid of anyone who was low income.

"Thanks for the heads up, Amanda, but one kid in a college class saying we're going to close doesn't mean we are going to."

"Maybe. But this place is always dead. How long do you think we can stay open like this?" She stood up. "Don't tell anyone I told you, okay? I'll see you later."

Stacey watched her go, suddenly feeling wide awake. Even though she had sounded confident to Amanda that they weren't going to close, the girl had a point. Business had been awful lately. How long would they really be able to stay open?

Maybe it was time to find another job. The only reason Stacey had stuck around there for so long was how flexible the hours were. Few places would accommodate Stacey like that. But if this place was going to close, she may have to put some applications out.

She sighed and rubbed her forehead, fending off a headache. Just another worry to add to her long list.

If you enjoyed this sample then look for **Love Invested – Persuasive Billionaire BWWM Romance Series, Book 1**.

Other Books by Shyla Starr

- Persuasive Billionaire BWWM Romance Series

- Tenacious Billionaire BWWM Romance Series

- Lonely Billionaire Romance Series

- Ardent Billionaire Romance Series

- Fervent Billionaire BWWM Romance Series

- Audacious Billionaire BWWM Romance Series

Get the latest update on new releases from the author at:

https://shylastarr.com/newsletter/

About the Author - Shyla Starr

Shyla currently specializes in writing interracial romance stories and is a huge fan of the alpha male. Simply put, there just aren't enough stories about mixed couple romances, which is something she is aiming to fix.

Being a bookworm all her life, when Shyla discovered men she also realized how easy it was to fulfill her fantasies through her writing.

When not writing and fantasizing about men, Shyla enjoys dancing, reading and chilling with her friends.

Connect with Shyla Starr

I really appreciate you reading my book! Here are my social media coordinates:

Friend me on Facebook:
https://www.facebook.com/shylastarrauthor

Follow me on Twitter: https://twitter.com/shylstarr

Check me out on Goodreads:
https://www.goodreads.com/author/show/8436084.Shyla_Starr

Subscribe to my newsletter:
https://shylastarr.com/newsletter/

Visit my website: https://shylastarr.com/

CPSIA information can be obtained
at www.ICGtesting.com
Printed in the USA
FSHW010505190221
78770FS